GWITHYAS

Door to the Void

to Annie for reading in the church

Isha Crowe

ISHA CROWE

www.kristell-ink.com

Paperback ISBN 978-1-911497-34-9
Hardback ISBN 978-1-911497-35-6
EPUB ISBN 978-1-911497-33-2

Cover art by Claire M. Carter
Cover design by Ken Dawson
Typesetting by Book Polishers

Kristell Ink

An Imprint of Grimbold Books
4 Woodhall Drive
Banbury
Oxon
OX16 9TY
United Kingdom

www.kristell-ink.com

TABLE OF CONTENTS

CHAPTER 1
Family Matters

An unearthly scream distracts me from my science magazine. I look up to check if anyone else has heard it. It seems not. Dad's still reading, Mum keeps browsing estate agents' websites, and my sisters continue their attempts to engage with the spirit world. The only one who reacts is a hairy orange spider the size of a sewer rat. It scurries over the desk from behind the computer monitor. I know that spider. It's been living here for ages. I looked it up on Google, but apparently this species does not exist. Not outside our house anyway.

Mum ignores the arachnid as well as the scream. She stares dreamily at the images on her screen and squeals, "Oh, look! Just look at this one! So bright, so new, so modern, so ordinary!"

She's almost drooling over her keyboard. I glance at the screen to see what she has spotted now. There's only a picture of a modern kitchen in a sunny family home, pretty similar to the others she tends to get excited about. I'm not really interested, but I feel sorry for her because no one, not even my father, ever pays any attention to her dream homes.

"Looks okay, Mum," I say.

"Okay?" she shrieks. "Okay, you call it? Oh, you're such a typical male. It's not merely okay. It's amazing! The ease of it all. There are doors on the cupboards. Beautiful smooth, shiny white doors. And a kitchen tap. See? An actual tap!"

"We have a kitchen tap," I point out.

Mum's smile freezes into an agonised grin, and she says, "Yes. I know. Wouldn't it be nice, though, if it was actually water that runs out of it?"

Most days it is, but I decide not to remind her of that. She's still upset about yesterday, when she'd wanted to do the washing up. One slight twist of the tap handle and half the kitchen had been covered in a sticky red goo. Poor Mum spent all evening trying to scrub the stuff off our dishes in the bath. I hadn't been too thrilled either, because it'd been my turn to clean the kitchen.

Mum clicks on streetview, another one of her favourites.

"Such charming surroundings too," she chirps when the images come up. "A park with healthy trees and real squirrels. And a school just around the corner."

A couple of clicks take her to the school's website, where she succumbs to cooing over a photo of a bunch of sugary-sweet-looking teenagers. They're dressed in summer uniforms and are smiling toothpaste-commercial grins over their tidy desks. Mum turns to my sisters, who are far too engaged in fiddling with their Ouija board to notice her, and she says, "Oh, you'd look absolutely adorable in those uniforms, my gorgeous darlings!"

Now there are many ways to describe my sisters. A kind, considerate person might say they're special, or unusual. Someone less friendly might call them weird, or ugly. A particularly bad-tempered individual, like the lady who works at our local chemist, could even say they are distorted little trolls. But no one, apart from my mother, would ever call them gorgeous.

My sisters have bulbous heads that are way too big for their emaciated bodies, eyes that resemble rabbit droppings, and lips that are so thin and dry that they remind me of parchment. They have no eyebrows or lashes, and their grey, wrinkly scalps boast only a few brittle tufts of hair. I reckon they must have an undiagnosed genetic disorder, because they don't actually look like girls; more like clumsily put together, nightmarish interpretations of human beings.

Not that I have a right to criticise. I may not be as surreal-looking as my sisters, but with my bony frame, greasy acne-skin and carrot-coloured hair I'm not quite an Adonis either. I also wear glasses that are so strong and thick that my eyes are barely visible behind them. I hate wearing them, but I desperately need to, as without them my visual world consists only of hazy blots and spots. I suppose I ought to be grateful for them. If only they didn't make me look like a complete dork.

Dad looks up from his book, a leather-bound volume on the mass production of thimbles, and says to my mother, "Why do you keep torturing yourself like this, Louisa? You know perfectly well that we'll never live in a place like that."

"I can dream, can't I?" says Mum without taking her eyes off the screen. "Ahh, and look at the price!"

I don't know how much the house costs, but I have no doubt that we can afford it, and probably several more like it. We have stacks of money. That's not the problem. There are other reasons why we cannot leave our run-down, leaky, mould-infested, smelly old manor. Pretty good reasons too, so unlike my mother I don't bother dreaming about living elsewhere.

Mum switches the computer off, rummages in her desk drawer and pulls out a brown velvet pouch.

"Time to tend to Nanny, dears," she says. "I think she may be feeling a bit unsettled tonight. I heard her call earlier."

So she did hear the scream after all. Or, as she puts it, the 'call'. My mother is the queen of euphemisms. She turns to my sisters and asks, "Is it your turn to help me, Amethyst?"

Amethyst's oversized head wobbles from left to right on her stick-neck. She keeps her eyes on the Ouija board. I can see the pointer move to the letter 'm', and wonder what messages from the other side my sisters pretend to be receiving now.

"His turn," mumbles Amethyst, gesturing in my direction.

"No it isn't!"

I'm lying. It is my turn. Amethyst went yesterday, with Dad, and Opal the day before, with Mum. But I have a headache, and I really don't feel like putting up with Nanny. She isn't even my real grandmother. My father's mother is dead, and my mother's mother lives somewhere in Australia, and we lost contact. Or, more likely, she is making sure that we never find her, so *she* doesn't have to take care of Nanny.

Mum puts on her pleading face and holds the pouch out to me.

"Oh, sweetie, I know it isn't your turn, but your sisters are playing so nicely at the moment, and you know that Nanny likes you. She once had a son of her own you know. He must have looked like you."

Huh. Before she ate him maybe. But I love my mother, so after a few grumbles I take the pouch and go with her anyway.

We leave the manor through the back door, and when we wade through the long grass another inhuman wail echoes over the lawn. It comes from the tower that stands dark, lonely and tall at the back of our garden, like a grim watcher guarding our equally grim family home. I suppose it was built by some ancestor who wanted to keep their family life in a state that resembles normality, because in this tower resides the aberration that is Nanny, tucked away in a room at the top, like a geriatric horror-version of Rapunzel, up seven flights of stairs. Stairs that are exceptionally steep and narrow, more like a ladder really, and the tower has no windows. It's like clambering up a chimney. Or at least I imagine it is. I've never actually been inside a chimney. I'm not Father Christmas after all.

Mum and I are quiet while ascending the stairs, mainly because we'd get out of breath if we tried to speak. I'm clutching the pouch, and its contents press into my palm. It contains five candles and five gemstones. Not proper precious gems, mind you. Those are the cheap kind that you can get from any online New

Age shop, but Mum adores them. She says they are gorgeous, just like my sisters and me. She's not exactly objective where her children are concerned. She calls us her little gems, and when we were born she insisted on naming us after the stones in the pouch. My father had other ideas. He thought we needed good, solid old-fashioned names. Because we are triplets, he thought it'd be a good idea if we all had the same first letter. I disagree with him on that, but back then I obviously didn't have any input.

My parents came to a naming compromise when my sisters and I were four months old. All that time we'd been officially nameless. The decision was that our first names, our official names, would be our father's choice. Sadly, his idea of good, solid old-fashioned names turned out to be Peregrine for me, and Perpetua and Presencia for my sisters. Our middle names would be for everyday use. My mother's choices. She named my sisters Amethyst and Opal. I got the really raw deal, not even a proper gem, merely a tiny glittery stone that is generally used to glamorise cheap jewellery. I have to live with being called Zircon. Peregrine Zircon Gwithyas, that's me. I'm sixteen years old.

When we reach the last step of the ladder-staircase, Mum knocks on the bolted wooden door, but she doesn't wait for an answer before unlocking the door, pushing it open and peering into the tower room while calling, "Nanny dearest, it's us! Time for your ritual!"

She walks in and I shuffle after her. The room is small, round, and as windowless as the stairs. The walls are bare black stone, the floor dark wood. A pentagram has been scorched out in the timber. Nanny's rocking chair in the middle is the only piece of furniture in here. Nanny doesn't need anything more. She doesn't walk or lie down. She only ever sits and rocks.

From where I'm standing, in the doorway, everything looks fine. Just a frail little old lady, knitting away in her rocking chair. Only when I move closer I see that heavy metal chains are holding her in that chair, that the knitting needles are actually her yellow, overgrown fingernails, and that what she is knitting is not wool, but her own matted, greasy, grey hair.

She raises her head and looks at me. Her flickering yellow eyes bore into my short-sighted ones and make me feel dizzy. I stagger, and Nanny grins. I guess I should be thankful that she has no teeth. But she does have a tongue, a purple double-pointed thing that slits in and out between her cracked lips as she speaks. "Hello dearie, nice of you to visit your old Nan. Come a little closer, will you? Come to Nanny so she can give the little boy a nice kissie kiss."

I start walking towards the rocking chair. I don't want to, but I can't control my legs. Mum quickly slips between me and Nanny.

"Now now, Nanny," she tuts. "You know very well that we don't do that. No kissing the children."

My dizziness fades and my legs work normally again. When I stop walking, Nanny hisses in disappointment. Her tongue, now almost as long as my entire arm, lashes out in Mum's direction.

"You filthy maggot-riddled piece of . . ." Nanny starts, and Mum quickly throws a handful of sneezing powder over her.

"Nanny, you really need to mind your language when the children are around!" While Nanny retches and puffs small clouds of sulphuric smoke from her wrinkled nostrils, I open the velvet pouch, and we start the ritual.

We do the ritual every evening now. It used to be once a week. Dad says that when he was a boy it was only every fortnight. My parents are not sure why it is so much more often now, but it worries them. I heard them talk one night.

"What if we need to do it twice a day next year?" Mum had asked.

"Then we will do so," Dad had said.

"Or three times a day? Or every hour?"

"We will perform the ritual as often as we can."

"We wouldn't have a life of our own anymore!"

Dad sounded severe when he said, "If we don't perform the ritual, no one on this entire world will have a life anymore."

I think Dad was exaggerating. Sure, I can see that Nanny is a nasty piece of work, and I'm convinced that she'd be quite capable of killing Mum, Dad, Opal, Amethyst and me. But not everyone in the entire world. I tried asking Dad about it. He told me to enjoy my childhood.

Mum chants. I hand her the golden candles and she lights them while I take the gems out of the pouch and place one on each point of the pentagram. The largest gem is a sapphire, and then there is a ruby. The others are—obviously—an opal, an amethyst and a zircon. An orange zircon. It matches my hair. Perhaps that's what inspired my mother to name us after the stones. I guess I should count my blessings; at least there's no carnelian.

I put the last gem in its spot and then we go to the centre of the room, each on one side of Nanny, who is by now totally enraged. Or agitated, as Mum calls it. Nanny always becomes agitated when we perform the ritual. She hisses and shrieks, and tries to strike us with her tongue. Mum and I don't look at her while we recite the words:

Gwitha sallow
Gwitha daras klos
Gwitha koeg yn tour gwag
Gwitha sallow ha krev tour bywnans
Gwitha gywnans yn fyw
Gwitha krev
Gwitha sallow

I know those words so well that I don't even have to think about them, and yet I don't know what they mean. I think they're Cornish, or some odd local dialect of Cornish. I considered looking them up online, but this chanting gives me a headache as it is, and I don't want to think about the words outside this room.

After we finish saying the last word, Nanny shudders and her eyes fall shut. Her tongue slithers back into her mouth. She mutters a bit, incomprehensible murmurings of a person in a deep sleep. Mum strokes Nanny's hair.

"Poor woman," she says.

I tidy away the objects while Mum covers Nanny with a soft blanket. Then she yawns and says, "I'm going to take a nap, Zircon."

She always takes a nap after our visits to Nanny. She says it's climbing the stairs that wears her out, but that's rubbish. It's the ritual that takes its toll on her. No, that too is rubbish. It's our whole life that's getting to her.

CHAPTER 2
Teachings

I OFTEN WONDER: WHY US? I CAN TELL THAT WE'RE NOT YOUR average people. My sisters, clearly, are not at all ordinary people. If they even are people at all. But Mum is fairly normal, only a little foggy at times, and I'm just a little dorky. Okay, a lot dorky, but that's not abnormal. Dad's always gloomy and miserable. He hardly ever smiles, and he never leaves the house, not even when Mum, the girls and I all go to town.

We went to town yesterday. Mum doesn't like leaving Dad, but we had to go because of me. I need to have my eyes checked regularly. I hate going for eye tests, because I usually end up with stronger glasses, looking even more dorky than before. At least the optometrist is nice. Ms. Chen is a thirty-something woman with short black hair and glasses almost as thick as mine, and she's always telling my mother that I am such a sweet, mature, bright lad, and that I'm her favourite patient. Yesterday she was especially excited, as for the first time since she started testing me my eyes had not gotten worse. That was a relief. I had calculated that if my vision continued to deteriorate at the rate it had done over the last ten years I'd be blind by the age of twenty-two, and I hadn't been too thrilled at that prospect.

"Actually," said Ms. Chen, studying my test results, "there is some indication that your left eye may have improved a little. Not enough to change your prescription, but I do think we should have the next test a few weeks early."

She gave me a warm smile, which made me feel as if I had achieved something to be proud of, and then turned to Mum to make the appointment.

Our next stop was the library, where I browsed the shelves to select an assortment of scientific literature and my sisters selected volumes dealing with the occult. Once we were done we made our way to the chemist to get Dad's medication. I'm not certain what he takes because Mum makes sure that I never get a chance to read the labels, but I suspect that they are mood enhancers. Yesterday the apothecary assistant confirmed my suspicions. While Mum swept numerous boxes of pills into her handbag, the assistant twisted one of her platinum-blonde curls around her long pink fingernail and said, "So the sunny autumn hasn't improved the old nutter's mood, has it?"

Mum's shoulders went rigid, but she sounded neutral when she said, "I'd like some ointment as well, please."

"What ointment would that be?" inquired the apothecary assistant.

"The usual," replied Mum, and she pointed at my sisters, who were lurking somewhere behind a display cabinet with poisonous substances. "For their eczema."

The apothecary assistant removed something distasteful from between her bleached teeth and sniggered, "Won't work, love. What they got ain't eczema, and I don't sell anything that works on scales."

"Please just give me the ointment," insisted my mother in clipped syllables, and the apothecary assistant did.

The way back from the chemist to the foot of the hill is always the worst part. It leads past a fish'n'chips shop that serves as a hangout for local youths. Yesterday a group of about ten kids had been standing in front of the shop. They were around my age and clearly very conscious of the latest trends in fashion.

When we approached they ceased their animated conversation to stare at us. Mum didn't notice. She was gazing at the clouds and humming Beethoven's Third. My sisters slithered along immediately behind her, oblivious to everything but their own twisted thoughts. I was last, and the only one of our family who registered the smirks and humiliating words.

"Freaks," giggled a tall, thin, blonde girl. "Loonies," said a chubby Asian kid who had a skateboard tucked under his arm.

I shuffled past, my shoulders hunched, when suddenly a fashionably booted foot popped out from the small group and tripped me up. I managed to keep my balance but couldn't prevent my library books from plummeting on the pavement. The teenagers laughed out loud when I fell to my knees to collect my reading material, and one of them said, "They should be locked up, that lot."

When I'd gathered my books I stood up and looked down the street. My mother and sisters were already turning the corner, totally unaware of what had happened. I rushed after them, but just before I also turned the corner, I looked back at the teenagers. They were chatting and laughing again. The tall girl was leaning closely against the chubby boy. They had already forgotten us.

I didn't forget them. I thought about them all the way home, wondering why it is that I'm so different. Perhaps it is because I have such a different life. Perhaps, if I lived like those kids, with a normal family in a normal town house, I'd also be eating fast food, skateboarding, chatting up girls and listening to the latest pop music while wearing designer-labelled clothing and a flashy haircut with colour wash.

I asked Dad about it that evening. He shook his head. "No, Zircon. You'd never be normal. You are a Gwithyas."

And that was it. He wouldn't speak of it any more. That's what he always does when I ask him about our family issues: give vague answers that make me even more curious, and then go silent on me.

To get from our wide, dark hallway into the sitting room you need to go through a small entrance hall. Mum reckons this is some posh statement from when the manor was first built, and the hall used to have a mirror and dressing table so people could tidy themselves up before entering the main room. Things are less sophisticated now. The hall is crammed full with cardboard boxes that contain useless objects that my father refuses to throw away, and I have to shuffle sideways to reach the double doors that lead into our sitting room. When I open the door I'm greeted by a murky odour of damp and rotting wood. The habitat in our sitting room is better suited for fungi than for human beings. It's a dark, decrepit space with only one tiny window. The furniture looks as if it has been zapped here directly from the Victorian era, or from even longer ago. I'm not that skilled at dating antiques.

Dad sits in his favourite chair near the window. Next to him a cup of no doubt cold tea balances on the edge of a wonky little side table which has decorated tiles on top. The pictures on the tiles have virtually disappeared between cracks, chipped edges and ingrained dirt. It's probably better that way. The one tile that is still in a reasonable condition shows an image of a young girl holding a plate full of severed fingers in a sauce of blood. No wonder Dad always lets his tea go cold.

Dad browses through a book. Still those thimbles. I fail to see how they can possibly be of interest to anyone, but my father seems fascinated. He frowns, nods and mutters to himself while he flicks the pages. Next to him a tall, once beautiful standing lamp struggles to pierce the eternal twilight with its insufficient 60-watt bulb.

Just behind the reach of its beam are my sisters, kneeling on the miserable excuse for a carpet, still playing with their Ouija board. No one acknowledges my presence, so without saying a word I sit down behind the computer. Only Mum and I ever use it. My sisters have never been interested, and Dad reckons it's evil. I think part of his brain must be from the same era as most of our furniture. I switch the computer on and rotate in the swivel chair while it loads.

I don't even know what I'm going to do on it yet. Maybe play online games. I play mostly puzzle games and shooters. I think I would enjoy MMORPGs, but Mum says it's not healthy to lose yourself in a fantasy world. It's no big deal though. The games are not important. What I do mostly on the computer is educate myself. My sisters and I don't attend school, and my parents have been less than conscientious with home-educating us, so the only ways I can gain some kind of academic proficiency are the occasional trips to the library and on the internet, where I read scientific articles and take part in academic forum discussions. I like that. Intellectual, rational discussions are rare in my house. Here, any hint of logic is instantly drowned in an ocean of wild superstitions.

My parents don't believe in any gods, that much is clear, but they do believe in a vast range of other, equally irrational things. Like Nanny. I mean, it's not that I don't believe in her; she is obviously here. But Mum and Dad reckon she is some sort of supernatural phenomenon. I don't. I used to, but now that I'm older and have access to more objective information, I have changed my mind. I now think that Nanny has a health issue. Dementia I suppose, and the purple colour of her tongue could be caused by a blood disorder.

I once posted on a forum about Nanny. That didn't go down well, most other members accused me of trolling, and the ones that did take me seriously suggested that I should report it to social services. They claimed it's not acceptable to keep a sick old woman tied up in an outbuilding. They have a point. But I couldn't report my own parents, could I? If I let social services barge in here, they'd take Nanny away, stick my parents in prison and me and my sisters in care. Quite a sacrifice, and who is to say Nanny will be better off in a nursing home with only overworked, underpaid care assistants to look after her?

And then, what if my parents are right after all? I don't believe that, and I shouldn't even consider the possibility, but it's hard to shake off an entire childhood of indoctrination. So I can't help imagining what would happen with all of us imprisoned and fostered. There'd be no ritual and Nanny might end up devouring the care assistants and all the other senior citizens in the nursing home.

I simply can't risk it.

And there is something else. Another reason that I don't want the outside world to know about Nanny. Perhaps she hasn't got dementia. Perhaps those teens in town, and people like the apothecary assistant, are not so far off the mark with their insults. My family's genetic makeup could very well be harbouring a predisposition to some sinister mental disorder.

If that is the case, I too may be affected. I keep envisioning this scene from the film 'One Flew Over the Cuckoo's Nest' where some dopey fellows in cotton pyjamas are sitting against a white wall. I don't want to end up like that. I don't want to spend my life in a mental institution.

There is nothing new on the forums, and with my headache I don't feel like deciphering an entire article, so I switch the computer off. As soon as the screen turns black I'm bored. Mum is still upstairs, Dad is reading his dull book, and my sisters are deeply engrossed in the escapades of their Ouija planchette. Amethyst looks up when I twist on my chair.

"We're speaking to a most interesting spirit," she tells me.

"The spirit wants to talk to you, Zircon," adds Opal. "Do you want to join in?"

Amethyst pats on the floor beside her. "Come."

Why not? It beats getting nauseated from over-swivelling. I sit down next to Amethyst and put my fingers on the cursor.

"Ask something," urges Opal.

I have done this before. I think it's silly, but it's one of my sisters' favourite games. Dad has made them their planchette. It's a flat bit of wood with three tiny legs, a big hole in the middle and another smaller hole through which you can stick a pencil. If you put your fingers on the wood, you can supposedly call a ghost, and it will reply by either writing with the pencil, or by steering the cursor over the Ouija letter board to spell words.

Apparently, the 'spirit' they are speaking to now is a writer. There are loads of scribbled-on pieces of paper scattered around the room. I don't believe in ghosts. I think Opal and Amethyst are steering the planchette themselves. I ask a question anyway.

"Who are you?"

Immediately, the wood rushes over the paper. I can barely hold my fingers on it, because it goes so fast.

'Never mind who I am,' writes the spirit. *'It is my message that is important. I shall only give it when asked by the last Guardian.'*

I look at my sisters. They are totally focused on the wood, their beady eyes shining with concentration.

"Ask!" hisses Opal.

"Ask what?" I say. "He said he needs a Guardian! A guardian of what? All I ever guard is my bedroom, to prevent you two from . . ."

Opal turns to me and snarls, "Zircon! Do as I say! Ask!"

I cross my arms and pull a face at her. "If you're gonna be like that . . ." I start, but I am interrupted by Dad. I hadn't noticed that he's standing right behind me.

"Ask," he whispers in a hoarse voice. "Please, Peregrine Zircon. Ask for the message."

This is remarkable. Dad has never interfered with this game before. I put my fingers on the planchette.

"All right, what is your message?"

The wood flies from under my fingers. Even Opal and Amethyst cannot hold on to it. There it goes. All by itself. No steering from my sisters, nothing. It rushes over the paper, writing wide curly letters:

'she is feeble she is losing her strength the door will open the koeg are coming coming for the gwithyas we waited for so long so long and now our

time is nearly there we shall come we shall crush the gwithyas we shall sow fear and pain and we shall reap death'

The planchette stops after writing the 'h' of death, and all I can think is that there were no capitals, full stops or commas. Don't spirits do punctuation? I fold my arms around my body and shiver. I'm cold. Behind me, Dad is eerily quiet. Opal and Amethyst put their fingers back on the wood. They wait a few seconds before shaking their big heads.

"Gone."

Dad walks off without saying anything. Typical. My sisters sit on the floor, close together, their stick-legs crossed, and they stare at me.

"What was that all about?" I ask.

Amethyst shrugs. Opal looks away.

"Come on, tell me. How did you pull it off? I know it was a trick. You can fool Dad, but not me."

"It wasn't a trick," says Opal.

"Don't be silly, Opal. You know I don't believe in ghosts. I don't even think you really believe in them yourself."

Opal shakes her head. "Not ghosts. Not ghosts." she says, and Amethyst explains, "They are not ghosts, no. That would be silly. They are souls, or they are Koeg, and they are in the Void, where we are wise and beautiful."

"In your dreams," I say.

Amethyst blinks, or what passes for that: her pale, lash-less eyelids slide over her bead-eyes and back. "Yes, indeed! How did you know?"

Opal pokes her. "He was using figure of speech, you silly goblin."

"Oh."

Amethyst would've blushed if she'd been a normal girl, but blushing requires blood to flow through the veins in your cheeks. I'm not sure if my sisters even have blood. Or veins. So Amethyst just looks at her feet and mutters, "Just because you cannot see it doesn't mean it is not there."

I get up and pull a face at the girls. "You two are as mad as Nanny!" I say, and I walk off, after Dad.

I know where he went. He always goes to the same place when he needs to think: his office. It's at the end of the main corridor, behind a narrow brown door that could use some fresh paint. That goes for everything in the house really. Nothing in here has been painted for as long as I've been alive, probably longer, and nothing ever will; it's just not worth the effort. I knock. Nothing. I knock again.

"Dad?"

"Is that you, Zircon?"

"Yes."

"Come in then. Just you though, no one else."

Hm. I wonder what brought on this bout of paranoia. I open the door. It creaks and squeaks and echoes loudly through the empty corridor, and I think I ought to come back later to oil the hinges. Or no, I shouldn't. These noises of deterioration at least prepare one for what is behind the door.

Dad's office is a mess. The walls have lost every trace of paint or plasterwork ages ago and on the wobbly floor there's only just enough space for a large, rusty metal desk, a lopsided leather chair, a rickety stool and a floor-to-ceiling woodworm-infested bookcase. Whenever I go in here, I always make a quick risk assessment of the state of that bookcase. Today it doesn't look as if it will collapse just yet, so I enter the room and shut the door. Dad is standing near the window. He is pretending to stare out of it, but the glass is so filthy that this is simply not possible.

"What happened just now with the Ouija, Dad?" I ask.

He turns around, tapping his leg. "It's time we had a talk, Zircon. A very serious talk. I was hoping I could keep it from you for a bit longer, so you would have a childhood free of worries, but it is not to be. Things are turning foul sooner than I anticipated, and I have no choice. You need to know."

Finally. Dad and his delusions. Did he really think that growing up in this house, with this family, I'd be worry-free? Knowing what the hell is going on in our lives can only make me feel better. Also, I'm not a child anymore. I sit on the desk, which, being metal, is marginally less likely to crumble to bits than the wooden furniture in this room, and I say, "Great. Tell me everything."

Dad sinks into his leather chair, shaking his head. His eyes are suspiciously watery when he says, "Yes, I shall tell you."

Then he stares blankly past me for at least two minutes. I wait, not quite patiently, until he finally starts speaking.

"Our family are not ordinary people," he says. "In fact, not all of us are actually people."

"Opal and Amethyst?" I ask.

Dad frowns at me. "Don't pick on your sisters, Zircon. They are obviously human. Not very common humans, I admit that, but human nonetheless."

I shrug. If he wants to think that, fine. He is their father after all. Dad stares at the wall for a bit before continuing his lecture, "Yes. The thing is, there is something here, in this house, something monstrous, something gruesome and horrendous."

"Nanny, you mean?"

"Stop interrupting me, Zircon. And no, I don't mean Nanny. I'll come to her later. This house, it was built by our ancestor, Graham Gwithyas, in 1613. Before he built it, this hill had been a site of Pagan worship, probably the only one that was still active in that era of Christian dominance. No one had dared to meddle with the old religion—not here, not where the forces are so strong. You ought to know about that. It is as good a place to begin as any. Listen."

Dad examines first the cobweb-infested ceiling and then the layer of dust on the floor before saying, "This is about our Earth's natural force."

"Gravity?" I suggest.

My father shakes his head. "No, Zircon. I do not mean gravity. I mean magic." He waits until I'm done uttering my derisive snort and continues, "It doesn't matter what you think, it's a fact that magic is everywhere. And in some places—only a handful—the force of magic is so strong, so concentrated, that it can even be used by human beings. This hill is such a place. The soil here, and the granite underneath, it's all steeped with the powers of nature." He rubs his temples. "Nature's magic is wild and unformed, and difficult to control. Most people are incapable of using it. A few, like the Pagan priestesses and priests, master the craft, but only after decades of study and practice. That's a good thing, because powers like this ought to be controlled by skilled, responsible individuals. Yet it is not always that way. Once every four or five centuries an individual will be born into this world with a natural ability to use magic. A natural witch or warlock, usually a member of a magical family. Graham Gwithyas was such a natural warlock."

"But we are not a magical family," I interrupt.

"Oh, but we are, Zircon," says my father. "Magic runs in our blood. It is not as powerful as it was in Graham, but it's there. My mother had it, and her brothers. I have it, you have it, your sisters have it."

"But not Mum?"

"No, not your mother. She has other, equally important special talents. I will tell you about those another time. Now where was I? Oh yes. Graham Gwithyas." Dad wrings his hands. "If only he had listened. The villagers tried to warn him, but Graham was a man of science, and had little patience with what he considered to be superstition."

Aha. I must take after Graham then.

"He built a home here," says Dad. "For himself and his beloved wife Sophie. It was here that his son Angus was born. It was Angus who later stopped his father's madness. He and the witch, Merryn Grenville. She is Nanny."

"Nanny?"

That's madness. She'd be centuries old.

"Yes," says Dad. "She was a priestess of the old Pagan religion. She warned Graham, but he wouldn't listen, and when the Koeg came all he could think of was power. A power he couldn't control. It are his sins we are still paying for."

Dad wriggles in his chair, taps the armrest and shakes his head. He's worrying me. He's acting even weirder than usual. And who or what is a Koeg?

"Graham was an evil man," says Dad while pulling a face as if he has cramp. "So many died because of him. Innocent people. His servants, and even his own wife. I've seen the corpses, now nothing but white bones. Never buried. Still here, and they always will be. Just like the doorway."

Dad shuts his eyes and moans. Perhaps he really has cramp. I'm getting more worried now, and am considering calling Mum when he opens his eyes and points at an open drawer in his desk. "Look in there, Zircon."

I do. It's full of pens, pencils, erasers, staples, pins and other stationery.

"What do you need?" I ask.

"Nothing, son, nothing. I want to show you something. You shouldn't mention this to anyone. Not to your sisters, not even to your mother." He sighs. "Especially not to your mother. I don't know what she'd do if she knew I told you. This stays between you and me. Now reach into the drawer."

I do as he says. This is kind of cool. A secret, just for Dad and me, for the Gwithyas men.

"All the way to the back," says Dad. "Can you feel the back?"

I can. It's cold and hard, as can be expected from a metal drawer.

"Now let you fingers slide along the back until you find a small chain. It should be near the top left corner."

I slide my fingers along the cold metal and shake my head. "I can't feel it."

"Keep searching!" Dad says. "It's supposed to be hard to find."

I run my fingers over the top left of the drawer back and then I feel a tiny chain, thin and delicate, like a necklace. "Got it."

"Good. Now pull it. Hard."

I pull. With a loud click the drawer shoots out of the desk and into my stomach. I almost tumble backwards, but the office is so cluttered that there is no room to fall, and I end up slumped against the bookcase.

"Sorry, Zircon," says my father. "I should've told you to step aside. Are you all right?"

"I'm fine."

I stand up and look at the desk. The back of the drawer has come loose, revealing a hidden compartment. Two tiny orange spiders rush out from it and hide behind a marker pen. The compartment is filled with sheets of papers.

"Take the documents out," Dad says. "Take them, and read them."

I carefully pull the pile of paper out and browse through it. Some of the documents are obviously very old, yellow with handwritten text on them, but there are also modern, computer-printed A4s. I pick out one of the old ones. It is elegantly handwritten, and far too small to read. For me anyway. I hold it up to Dad.

"What does it say?"

Dad ignores the document, mumbles something I cannot quite understand, runs his fingers through the papers and pulls out a white A4 sheet.

"Here." He hands it to me. "I typed this out for you, because I knew you wouldn't be able to read the original. I also modernised the language." He puts a hand on my shoulder and says, "This document, Peregrine Zircon, will change your life. And not for the better. I'm sorry, son."

He has tears in his eyes. I don't like the idea of seeing my father cry. Better get reading. I push my glasses up and hold the paper in front of them. It reads:

'Instructions for the firstborn Gwithyas'

That would be me. I'm four minutes older than Opal and five than Amethyst. Big Brother Zircon. The instructions start with a short note.

'Cursed I am, and all those who descend from me, yet blessed, for it is the Gwithyas who protects the hill, the town, the county, the kingdom, and yes, the entire world. We, and the witch who is the lock, none are more important than us. The world depends on me, on her, and on you, my descendant.

Angus Gwithyas.'

Odd note. Whiffs of megalomania. I read on.

'Instructions, written by Angus Gwithyas.

You shall keep the door shut, so the Koeg cannot enter our world.

You shall wed the one appointed to you by the enchanted family tree, for this person is bound to you by the Earthen force and shall be your shield.

You and your spouse shall live in the Gwithyas manor, for that is where the force dwells.

You and your spouse shall have at least one child. The Gwithyas bloodline has to be maintained. If it is broken, the Koeg will be free and the world will be doomed.

You and your spouse, and later your children, shall learn the ritual, as described in these documents.

You and your spouse, and later your children, shall perform this ritual as often as required, for it is the ritual that channels the magic of the hill.'

Next is a page that describes the ritual that we so often perform. I don't read it yet. I look at Dad, but he turns his face away from me. Is he still being tearful? How gross. He sighs heavily and whispers, "I am sorry, Zircon. I would have loved to give you a normal life. But you are a Gwithyas. A Gwithyas born at the most unfortunate time. It is so much worse now. So much."

He turns around to face me. No tears. His face is dark and grim. His eyes seem black instead of their usual bland grey. He grinds his teeth and his hands are shaking.

"It is a curse, Zircon," he grunts. "But it is also a great honour. For Angus was right, it is us, the Gwithyas family, who are the most important people in the world. Ah, my boy, you have no idea."

No, I don't. Those documents are all nice and well, but so far they only managed to confuse me and make me doubt my father's sanity. I open my mouth to ask for a proper explanation, but before I can utter a sound Dad takes the papers off me, flaps them around and says, "Not even Angus fully understood the significance. Not even he. Or perhaps he did. Perhaps he did not want to accept it."

He places the documents back into the secret compartment. Just before he puts the drawer back the way it was I spot something shiny at the back of the hidden compartment. Dad shuts the drawer, stands up and straightens his back.

"I know the truth, Zircon," he says. "And now you will too. We, the Gwithyas family, we are the Guardians of the Gates of Hell."

Hell? I brace myself for more far-fetched revelations, but Dad looks at his watch—one of those silver things on a chain, another ancient family heirloom—and gasps. "So late already! I need to start cooking!"

He ushers me out of his office and disappears in the direction of the kitchen. I still don't know anything.

Dad has cooked up a quick curry, and we're all sat at the dinner table, chatting away as usual. When I say as usual that means that only Mum is chatting. Dad eats in silence and looks depressed. Opal and Amethyst poke their forks into their food and gather undesirable bits on the edges of their plates. They're very picky eaters. Today I don't eat a lot either. I'm thinking. That first instruction, '*you shall wed*', sounds suspiciously like an arranged marriage. I ought to be disgusted by such an oppressive, outdated concept, but if I'm honest I rather fancy the idea. I've seen enough of the outside world to know that no self-respecting modern female would ever want to date a misfit like me. An arranged marriage might be my only chance to ever get a girl.

"Aren't you eating, Zircon, love?" asks my mother. "Don't you like it? You're not sick, are you?"

I shake my head and quickly stick a spoonful of rice in my mouth. It's hot. Hot as in overly spicy, and while my tongue burns and I break out in red-skinned sweatiness, I remember my Dad's words: Guardian of the Gates of Hell. Dad was getting a bit carried away there. I don't believe hell exists. Or heaven for that matter. I am a fervent atheist. I know that there are no such things as gods, evil spirits and curses. All superstitious rubbish. The scientific mind only believes in what the world clearly shows it. But I am confused too. I'm not sure what my world is clearly showing me. On all my intellectual online forums no one ever mentions orange spiders. Or red goo coming from the tap. Or subhuman sisters. Or, of course, Nanny.

So I can see where Dad is coming from. Nanny, with her ghoulish appearance and miserable attitude, surely resembles something made by the devil. I've seen horror films, even though our internet connection is too slow and unreliable to download full films. There's still the telly, and the film library is just at the bottom of the hill so I can rent DVDs without even having to go through town. I've always been allowed to rent and watch whatever I wanted, even the most repulsive 18-plus horrors. Mum and Dad aren't interested in age ratings, and the skinny, smelly guy who runs the film library is too depressed to care about anything. Anyway, from those films I have learned that people imagine their demons to be a lot like my Nanny. Of course demons don't actually look like anything because they don't exist. But Nanny exists. And so does her tongue. Which is purple because of a blood disorder, or so I reasoned, but then why is it so long? And how do those spiders fit in? And the ritual? It doesn't add up. No matter how much I ponder on it, it never does. My brain is going in overdrive, and the spicy curry stirs unpleasantly in my stomach. I drop my fork, mumble, "Need the loo," and dash away. No one argues. I don't really need the loo, although I have a nagging suspicion that I'll have to run for it later. I just wanted to be alone. And I want answers, and now that my entire family is having supper, I can get into Dad's office without anyone knowing.

The door isn't locked. Nothing in this house is ever locked. Not because we're such an open, trusting family, it's just that all the locks have rusted through years ago. I open the office door slowly and carefully. I don't think my family can hear the tormented squeals of the hinges all the way in the dining room, but I'm taking no risks.

Once inside the office I open the desk drawer, pull the little chain, get the documents out and search for the shiny object. There it is, stuck to the back of the secret compartment with sellotape. I peel the tape off and the object, a small metal key, falls into my hand. It looks like a perfectly ordinary key, and it has a tiny printed label taped around it. I hold the label close against my glasses, and only just manage to make out each letter. The first one must be a C, and then an E, and then… an I? Two I's? Then A-R. I get it now, those I's are L's, and the word is cellar. This is the key to our cellar. I didn't even know we had a cellar.

I stick the key in my pocket. I'll decide what to do with it later. Right now I want to find that enchanted family tree, but when I browse through the papers in the drawer it's not there. I'll have to ask Dad about it later. I have another browse through the documents to see if there's anything with letters large enough to read. I find a short, torn of bit of paper. It looks old, but not as old as the original instructions. Black ink on yellow paper, with little decapitated butterflies drawn to the left. The handwriting is messy, like a child's, and large enough for me to read. So I do just that.

'to nathaniel
i lokd the door you and mummi can not do the ritool now
my frinds wil com out to play it wil be fun
later i wil com for you and we can have diner
my frinds fink you wil tast nice
cecilia'

Odd child, that Cecilia. And terrible at spelling. I'm glad she's not my sister.

There are more letters in the drawer, but all are in tiny print and I can't be bothered to decipher them. I stick the papers back in the secret compartment, and two little orange spiders scurry into it as well. Where did they come from, so suddenly? I suppose they live in the drawer, so I wait until they are settled before I shut it.

CHAPTER 3
Strangers

NOW WHAT? ASK DAD ABOUT THE FAMILY TREE, OR TRY TO FIND the cellar? I reckon Dad has had enough stress for today, so I'll go to the cellar. That's not as easily done as said, since I only learned of its existence a few minutes ago and I have no idea where it is. Aren't cellars usually near kitchens? I mean, if you'd use them for food storage that'd make sense, wouldn't it? But then, the Gwithyas family does everything differently, and common sense is not one of our strongest personality traits.

Hoping that the manor was built in the traditional way, I go to the kitchen. No one is there. The dirty washing-up lies ignored in the cracked stone sink. Our kitchen is small, dark and scruffy, but not very old. Well, compared to the house it isn't. I think my grandparents had it installed, so it's still had a solid forty-odd years of service. Dad once told me that the original kitchen was much bigger, because back when the house was built people used to hang complete dead pigs from their ceilings. A huge space like that must be easy to find, but chances are that it's not here. Still, I have to start looking somewhere, so I look around. Yesterday I spent hours in the kitchen, scrubbing the results of the tap incident off the walls and ceiling and off the bolted door in the back wall. Come to think of it, a bolted double door is an uncommon feature in a family kitchen. I never thought of that, probably because I've never known it to be different. I've also never known this door to be open, there's always been a heavy padlock holding the bolt in place. I get the key out of my pocket and sure enough, it fits the padlock. I turn the key, the lock clicks and the bolt slides loose. I push the door open.

When my eyes have adjusted to the darkness I see a massive space with a black tiled floor and a colossal open oven built into the wall. This has to be the old kitchen. It's not actually a cellar, but since the key fitted the lock, I suppose it is, or was, used as one. And rightly so. It's freezing cold in here—great for storage.

I shiver when I walk towards the stone oven. It's so large that you could get a double bed in there, and the chimney that leads from it is wider than our shower cabin. When I look inside the oven my heart misses a beat. There's a skull in there. Not one of a pig, or a cow, or of any animal that people traditionally hack to bits to scorch into edible roast. This skull is unmistakeably human.

I shuffle my feet. The floor tiles are so cold that I feel their chill through the rubber soles of my shoes. I want to take another step but then I hear something, not sure what. I stay still to listen. No. It's only the clattering of my own teeth. I force myself to look at the oven again, and the skull's empty sockets gaze back at me, as if they blame me for their depressing situation. I shake my head. I'm being ridiculous. It's only a bit of bone that was once part of someone's body. Nothing to be afraid of. Closer, then.

There are more bones behind the skull, but I'm not certain from which creature they are. There are also more skulls, and those are all clearly human. What did Dad say again? Never buried. Still here, and they always will be. I'm shivering more now. It must be way below freezing point in here. There's that sound again! Definitely not my clattering teeth. These are voices, odd voices that are too quiet to make out what they are saying, yet sharp and vicious. I try to stick my fingers in my ears, but find that I can't feel them, and when I look at my hands they are lifelessly white.

The voices grow into whispers and I try to speak, to ask them what they are saying or what they want, but my mouth is too stiff. The whispers get louder still and become shrieks and screeches and giggles. There are words too, muddled and strange. I still can't make them out. I'm so cold.

Without wanting it, I look at the skulls again. Their fleshless, toothy jaws are moving up and down to the rhythm of the eerie voices, which holler through the oven and through the shaking skulls to me. Inhuman voices, inaudibly quiet yet louder than everything. Only them I can hear, those grating voices, slicing through me, through my ears, my eyes, my brain. My head pounds, my eyes burn, my body freezes. Now I understand the words: *"Die! Die! Die! We will rip you to shreds, Gwithyas! Tear out your insides, squash your eyeballs, hurt you hurt you, so you will die die die!"*

I want to cover my ears but I cannot move my arms. I try to cry out for help, but my mouth is ice, my words are gone and my voice is silent. Then I see the spiders, sparkling orange, and everything goes black.

I scream at the top of my lungs, and this time I succeed. I hear my own voice, full of terror and agony. A hand touches my cheek.

"Zircon! Zircon!"

I open my eyes and see two oval blurs hovering over me. Human faces. That's what they look like when I'm not wearing my glasses. I can just make out their eyes: one set is hazel brown and one set is pale grey. My parents' eyes. And there is light too. I am no longer in the old kitchen.

"Zircon?" That's my mother, sniffing away a sob after every word. "Zircon, sweetie, speak to me? Please?"

I want to touch her to reassure her so I raise my hand. There's an obstruction. A blanket, a soft, warm comforting blanket. I smile.

"He smiled!" Dad sounds hoarse and croaky, but that doesn't

stop him from bombarding me with questions. "Are you okay, boy? How do you feel? Are you hurting? Can you see me? Can you talk?"

"I'm fine," I say. My shaky voice contradicts that, but my parents sigh with relief. Then, of course, come the kisses. Mum can be pretty horrible like that. They land everywhere, on my cheeks, my nose, my eyes, and funnily, I don't even mind.

An hour later I'm still in bed. Dad has left the room shortly after I woke up, but Mum stayed with me and fusses over me in an embarrassing way, which is totally unnecessary. I'm a bit groggy, but otherwise fine, and I just want to get up and get on with things, but Mum won't hear of it. I've had three hot drinks in the last hour, and now she is trying to feed me soup.

"If you just give me that spoon I'll eat it myself, Mum," I say.

"Oh, no sweetie, you can't. Not yet. You're far too weak. Now have this soup. It'll make you feel better." She presses a spoon against my mouth, and I pull back.

"I really don't need to be fed," I insist. "I feel fine."

"One little spoonful for Mummy," says my mother, wriggling the spoon between my lips. "Go on, go on."

"Mum!" I push the spoon to the side so the soup spills over my duvet, and I jump out of bed.

"Zircon!" Mum slaps her hands over her mouth. "Oh darling, you really need to rest! Get back in bed, quickly, before . . ."

"Before nothing, Mum. I'm fine, really." I look down my body and am relieved to find that I'm still in my day clothes. My parents did not change me into my pyjamas. At least I was spared that humiliation.

"Zircon . . ." My mother's voice falters. I pat her hand.

"I'm okay, Mum, don't you worry. If you really want to make me feel better, explain to me what happened in the old kitchen. I don't understand."

I wait for her to answer, but she just sits there on the wicker chair and stirs in the soup.

"Fine then," I say. "I'll go ask Dad. Is he in his office?"

She doesn't look up, nor does she stop stirring the soup. In a quiet, flat voice she tells me that Dad is indeed in his office. She doesn't move when I walk away.

As I leave the room I bump into my sisters. Figures. They were listening at the door, curious little spies that they are. They look at me with their beady eyes wide open and their big wobbly heads slightly tilted. Opal is smiling. Now that's just wrong. My sisters never smile.

"Are you okay, Zircon?" asks Opal.

"We were concerned," adds Amethyst.

I say that I'm fine and walk past them. I tell myself that they were just curious, and that they annoy me, but deep down I know that they really were worried about me, and somehow that feels reassuring.

The office door is open and Dad is sitting at his desk, browsing through some papers. He squints. There isn't enough light in here. When I flick the light switch the office remains the same cold, trembling shade of grey as before. The light bulb must've died. Leave it to my father to sit in the dark rather than replace a burst bulb.

He has opened the window though. I didn't even know it could be opened. It's chilly outside this evening, so it's now also chilly in the office. Of course Dad hasn't noticed. He's too engrossed in his papers.

"Dad?"

He looks up and I get a shock when I see his face. I'm used to my father being depressed, but never before have I seen him look this miserable. His bloodshot eyes are rimmed with dark shadows as if he hasn't slept in weeks. His skin is so pale that it approaches grey, as if to match the office, and his lips appear slightly blue.

I shut the window and ask, "Are you all right, Dad?"

"I ought to ask you that question," he replies.

"I'm fine. You look terrible though. Why did you open the window? It's freezing!"

He gazes at the filthy glass of the window as if he has never seen it before in his life. "Ah," he mutters. "It is indeed cold. I didn't notice. I guess I wanted some fresh air. Thank you for closing it."

"That's all right," I say while moving away from the window to stand near my Dad. That was a bad idea, because he now reaches out and strokes my hand. That's creepy. Dad is never this affectionate.

"You were lucky today, Zircon," he says. "You have no idea how lucky. It's a miracle that you're still with us now. I cannot understand—how did you get out of there, boy?"

"Out? Well, you got me, didn't you?"

Dad shakes his head. "We heard you scream," he says, and he closes his eyes. "I can't tell you how horrible that was. Your mother and I were in our bedroom. We could hear you all the way there. We rushed downstairs, but we didn't think we'd find you alive. When we came into the kitchen your sisters were already there with you. You were unconscious, and the girls told us you'd come running from the old kitchen, and then collapsed."

Odd. I don't recall running at all. But then, the memory of that chilling experience in the old kitchen is already fading, and right now it seems as it was just a really bad dream. I'm starting to think that it was. It has to be.

"How did you get out, Zircon?" asks Dad again.

There is only one way I could have gotten out of a scary dream. "I woke up," I tell my father.

He frowns. "Woke up?" Then he nods. "Ah. I see. You are wrong there, Zircon. It wasn't a dream."

Not a dream? Sure it was. Either that, or I'm going mad. I stare at my feet. It occurs to me that I've been wearing these socks for three days. I ought to change them. Was it a dream or not? What do they call it again when you hear voices that aren't real? Auditory hallucinations, I think. Clinical descriptions of mental illnesses pop up in my memory, stuff I've been reading about online, hoping that I'd never recognise myself in them. Then, I didn't. But now… I think it was schizophrenia, with the hallucinations. A particularly nasty mental disorder, that. I'll have to look it up again.

Dad taps the armrest of his chair. "I blame myself for what happened," he says. "I should have told you everything. You need to be warned. You need to be prepared."

I don't ask what I need to be prepared for because I assume he'll tell me, and he does, in his own roundabout way.

"Things are changing," he says. "It's becoming more dangerous. There is a chance that soon you will be the Guardian, son. That is not good. Not at all good. You aren't ready." He taps the armrest more vigorously and mumbles, "I've had it easy. I was much older than you are now when the task became mine, and I was already married to your mother, who is my shield. And that is important because no Guardian can work alone. The forces we have to deal with are too great. We need the support, the care and the protection of our life partner. Otherwise the emptiness will destroy us."

Dad leans over to me, his eyes wide open. "The villagers called them the Koeg," he says, spraying droplets of saliva onto my face. "The empty ones, for they are empty, and their world is the Void, and the only thing that fills them up is the unbearable suffering of living beings. They were created in wrath, and wrath is all they are. If the Koeg come to our world, everyone and everything shall suffer, with death being the only way out. It happened before, Zircon. In the cellar, in the old kitchen. Graham called them, and they came, but he could not control them. The witch stopped them with her sacrifice. And now they are returning, when she is feeble. Remember, Zircon? That's what the spirits told us. She is feeble, and she won't last. And without her . . ." He grabs my hands and squeezes them a little too hard for comfort. His eyes are feverish and his voice is low when he says, "You cannot let them through, Peregrine

Zircon. No matter how great your own anguish—and it will be great—you'll have to endure it. You cannot let the Koeg through. Promise me you won't."

"I promise," I say, and to my relief Dad lets go of my hands. He stares into nothing and mutters, "The Void. The horror. My poor poor boy."

I think my father has lost it. Maybe I lost it too, because without wanting it I ask, "How do I stop them?"

Dad blinks, and looks at me as if I have just walked in. "Ah," he says. "Of course. Yes. I'll tell you what to do, son. Sit down. You need to be fully concentrated."

I get ready to set myself down on the wooden stool, but then I spot something large, moving slowly forward, and I realise how stupid I have been: I didn't check the state of the woodworm-infested bookcase when I entered the office. I shout a warning, but it comes too late. I have only just enough time to jump back before the ancient piece of furniture collapses on top of my father.

I don't know why Mum won't call a doctor. I even try to oppose her and reach for her telephone, but she is adamant and refuses to give it to me.

"It would only make matters worse, Zircon."

She whispers, as if speaking normally would take too much of her. Her hands are trembling as she straightens the blankets. I feel as sorry for her as for Dad, who is lying under those blankets, pale and unconscious.

Mum doesn't see the fat orange spider that scuttles over the sheets and then disappears under the bed. It's the one that lives behind the computer. What's it doing in here?

A ghoulish howl resonates over the garden into the room. Mum and I both look out the window, at the tower standing under the cold moon like a tornado frozen in time. Mum gives Dad a small kiss and stands up with a weary sigh. "It is time for the ritual."

I pull a chair to the side of the bed and gesture her to sit on it. "I'll do it," I say. "Dad needs you here, and you are too tired."

She opens her mouth to argue, and then shuts it again. She sinks into the chair, takes my father's limp hand in hers and doesn't look at me again. I hadn't expected that. Now I actually will have to do the ritual on my own. I'm not sure I can. I hesitate, but when I look at my mother she seems so tired and fragile that I can't bring myself to drag her up that horrible tower again. I have no choice. I'll have to do the ritual on my own.

When I turn to leave the room, my sisters are standing in the doorway.

"We will come with you," they say.

So weird. Just the three of us trotting through knee-high garden weeds to the tower, and then up the stairs to the round room. I enter first.

Nanny is dozing in her rocking chair, and her chains appear as sturdy and tight as ever. Opal and Amethyst are right behind me. They're quiet, but then, they never say a lot. Their small, ugly faces have no expression but I know they are as nervous as I am. My sisters. There for me when I need them most. Perhaps they are human after all.

I've taken the velvet pouch from Mum's desk. My fingers tremble when I open it. Opal and Amethyst hold hands and stay close to the door while I light the candles and place the gems.

Nanny wakes up and sees us.

"Well, well, little sweethearts. Did you come to visit your old Nan all by yourselves now? How sweet, how sweet, how very very sweet. Come closer, then."

Amethyst steps forward, her legs stiff, and Opal whimpers but doesn't let go of Amethyst's hand. Nanny's purple tongue zaps out of her mouth. Are my eyes playing tricks on me or does that wretched thing have three points now? Nanny cackles: an eerie, hollow sound. Amethyst walks, and even when Opal pulls her arm back, she keeps going, dragging Opal along. Nanny writhes in her chair and hisses.

"Come to Nanny, little girl. Come here for a kissie kiss!"

"No!" I say, and I position myself between Nanny and my sisters. What does Mum usually say again? "No kissing the children!"

It doesn't work. Amethyst keeps walking, Nanny keeps cackling, the tongue keeps flashing. I should've brought the sneezing powder. When Amethyst moves past me I hop forward so that I'm between her and Nanny again.

"No kissing," I start, but Nanny interrupts me: "Ohh, such a surprise, three for the price of one!"

Her voice is so sharp that it hurts my ears and I flinch.

"Stop her, Zircon!" Amethyst calls. She's still moving closer and closer to Nanny, with Opal pulling at her arm, and Nanny reaches out with one gnarled skeletal arm, her hook-like nails snapping like hedge-cutters. Opal screams and I shout at Nanny, "Stop! Stop it you nasty old hag!"

I didn't expect that to work, so I'm kind of baffled when Nanny stops snapping her nails and narrows her yellow eyes before screeching, "Old? It's not me who is old! You tricked me! Foul liars! I shall have the boy instead. His living, bleeding flesh!"

Her tongue bursts out of her mouth like a bright purple flame and hits me on the chest. I yelp with pain and tumble backwards over the floor. I roll over to my stomach and jump back on my feet, only to see the tongue coming at me like a bolt of purple cartoon-lightning.

Then they're there again. The spiders. Two of them, tiny and orange. They came from nowhere, and they know very well where to go next. Up Nanny's nose they run, and sure enough the rotten old bag stops cackling. She pulls the tongue in, sputters and wheezes, gasps and retches, and then sneezes, hurling two orange puffs from her enlarged nostrils.

Amethyst falls on the floor. Opal pulls her up and cries out, "The ritual! Zircon! Finish the ritual!"

As fast as I can I fling every gem onto its designated pentagram point, and I start reciting. My sisters join in.

Gwitha sallow
Gwitha daras klos

Nanny squirms in her chair. Her voice goes up, becomes louder, and she produces a screech that human vocal chords should not be able to produce. The room goes icy cold, and then it all comes back to me. The cellar, the voices, the words, and the cold. I shiver, and my teeth clatter while I continue to recite the enchantment.

Gwitha koeg yn tour gwag
Gwitha sallow ha krev tour bywnans
Gwitha gywnans yn fyw
Gwitha krev

Almost too cold now to speak. With great effort I push out the very last phrase:

Gwitha sallow!

As the last word is echoed by my sisters, Nanny convulses and growls in her chair, and her emaciated body appears to glow dark purple while her burning eyes crawl out of their sockets, and she screams. Her hollow wails crash into the room with such force that I'm flung against the wall. The air is whacked out of my lungs, and I slide down onto the wooden floor. As I lay there gasping for oxygen, I hear one of my sisters cheer, "Zircon! It worked!"

I'm not in a state to answer. I focus on getting my breathing going again, and once that works I re-adjust my glasses and look up. My sisters are both grinning at me, exposing their tiny pointed teeth. I wish they wouldn't do that.

"You did it!" says Opal.

"Did what?"

"The ritual of course," says Amethyst. "You did great. Look!"

She points at the rocking chair, where Nanny slumps, crumpled up into a frail little lady, quieter than ever. She snores a bit, mutters contentedly and her toothless mouth even shows something resembling a smile. I get up and walk over to her to see if her eyes have indeed popped out, which they haven't, and she just continues to sleep.

CHAPTER 4
Aches

I SIT AND I STARE INTO THE FIREPLACE. THERE'S NOTHING IN THERE but a small heap of charcoal, but I'm not really looking at that of course. I'm thinking. I still can't believe that my sisters and I did the ritual without our parents. It was a bit messy, certainly, but the effect has been much more powerful than usual, and it's not just Nanny who has calmed down: Mum is also picking up on it. When she came downstairs about an hour ago she was smiling and humming her favourite cheesy eighties song, and she told us that Dad is doing much better. She reckons he has a mild concussion and should be fine in a few days. She was still singing while cooking supper, and for the first time that I can remember she didn't burn the food.

Opal and Amethyst were a bit demure at first, but now that our evening meal is over they're on the old carpet laying their tarot cards and seem almost happy. Mum is behind her computer, looking at houses as usual, but right now our own house feels good enough. Cleaner somehow, more peaceful, and my family is obviously benefiting from it.

I'm not. My chest burns and itches. I checked it over earlier and there's a bright red mark where Nanny's tongue hit me, like a burn. I also have a splitting headache, my body is stiff and sore, and I've never felt so exhausted in my life. I didn't tell my family and during supper I pretended to be all happy, because I figured they need a break from their miserable lives, especially Mum. Who knows how long this weird lightness will last? Tomorrow everything might be as horrid as ever, or worse. But I can't keep up the pretence any longer, so I get up from my chair—even that is an effort; I feel like an old git—and I say, "I'm going to the office."

The office is a mess. Nobody has bothered to tidy up the collapsed bookcase, and since I have no intention of doing anything about it either, it'll have to stay this way for now. I tiptoe between the cracked shelves, shattered boards and snapped nails until I find the drawer with the secret compartment. It has popped out of the now mangled desk, and I need to push aside some rubble before I can pick it up to take to my room.

My room is the best place in our house. It's on the second floor, stretches over the entire width of the manor and has large windows to three sides: two overlook the garden, and one has views over the unmade hill-path towards town. I often look out of that window and imagine what it'd be like to be normal.

Right now it's a clear night so I can see the stars and the lights of the houses in town. I sit down in the comfy chair in front of the window and switch on my extra-bright reading light. I pop some painkillers in my mouth because my headache isn't getting any better, and then start skimming through the papers.

The first thing I examine is the description of the ritual. Nothing new there, it's exactly as we always do it. Light the candles, place the gems, chant the lines. It advises to stay clear of the witch. That must be Nanny. Curious. Dad also said she was a witch, but aren't witches supposed to do magic? Like turn you into a frog, or, if she's a good one, cure your illnesses? Nanny doesn't do anything like that. How then is she a witch? Perhaps 'witch' is also an ancient expression that means 'evil scary possessed old hag'. Never mind. Onto the next document: a letter.

Old, yellow paper that crumbles, so I have to hold it carefully. The first words, in elaborate old-fashioned handwriting, are: *'I will mourn you forever, my love.'*

I put it aside. Too labour-intensive to read, and way too depressing. At the moment I don't want to learn about the miserable fates of my pathetic ancestors. I feel bad enough as it is, and really don't need to be reminded of how hopeless our situation is, how impossible it is that Mum will ever live in the nice, sunny house she so desires, that my sisters will ever go to school, that Dad will ever smile. Or that I will ever live the life of a normal boy.

I put aside all the letters I find, one by one, until I stumble upon a thicker, folded piece of paper. I turn it over in my hands. Weird colour. Kind of white, but not quite. Weird texture too, so smooth, even shiny. A bit like the cover of a glossy fashion magazine, but even smoother than that, and sturdier. I've never seen anything like it. I unfold the paper—if that's what it is—to examine it better. It's large, somewhere near A3 I'd say. And it looks old.

The text on the document is handwritten, and not very neatly. There are inkblots and scribbles everywhere. In the middle is a crude drawing of a tree with lots of branches and side-branches. This must be that enchanted family tree. I wonder what is so enchanted about it; it looks like an ordinary drawing to me. Perhaps the enchanted part is that weird material it's drawn on.

I rearrange my reading light so it shines directly onto the drawing. I still can't read the words well. This isn't going to be easy, but I'm curious enough to put in a lot of effort. I start at the bottom, at the roots of the tree. Under the left root is one name: Graham Gwithyas. He lived from 1576 until 1624. In the other root Sophie Giselle Dubois, his wife. I never knew I had French blood in me. Je m'appelle Zircon Gwithyas. I snigger, which is just stupid because it's not that funny really, and then I study the tree further. Graham and Sophie had one son, Angus. That's the one who wrote the instructions. Next to Angus' name is a tiny image of a bolted door, which, according to the symbol key written under the roots, is the symbol of the Guardian, with a capital G. There are many Guardians in my family tree, at least one in every generation.

I follow the tree from Angus upwards, generation after generation, until I find my own name hidden near a scraggy twig at the top. Apparently I'm not as important as I'd hoped. Both Dad and I have the bolted door next to our names, and I have something else too. A faint line connects my name to another one, one that is not part of the tree, but shimmers at the side of the document, away from the family. I don't recognise the name. Joanna Egwueke. She was born fourteen months before me.

I remember the arranged marriage thing. Perhaps this girl is to be my wife. I smirk, think that I probably look completely stupid, sitting here alone, gazing at an ancient document with a wide grin on my face, but I keep smirking while I run my finger over the letters. Joanna. Not a bad name. Sounds kind of warm, loving, yet feisty. I wonder who she is, and what she looks like. Egwueke sounds foreign. African I'd say. I hope she's not actually living in Africa. That much distance between her and me would seriously compromise my chances of ever getting a love life.

I place the family tree on my lap and lean back to imagine our first meeting. I'll introduce myself, I'll say that I am Zircon Gwithyas, the Guardian, and I'll confidently stick out my hand, gently taking hers, and she will smile sweetly and a bit shyly, and she'll look at me with her eyes wide open and full of admiration.

Or not.

I take my glasses off, rub them clean on my sleeve and tell myself to not give in to such silly daydreams. Whoever this Joanna is, she'll probably take one look at my carrot hair and my distorting spectacles and run away in terror. I put my offending yet necessary visual aid back on, force Joanna out of my mind, and continue to study the family tree.

Enchanted or not, it sure is unusual. For one, it appears that all the children born to a Gwithyas get the surname of Gwithyas, even if their father has a different name. Nowadays it is fairly common for a child born in a marriage to get their mother's surname, but up until a few years ago it wasn't even possible, at least not outside my family. And another thing: according to this tree, my father has a brother. An older brother. Ronald Gwithyas. I never knew that. I always thought Dad was an only child. Ronald has the bolted door symbol next to his name, so he was a Guardian. Or he still is. It doesn't say here that he died. I wonder what became of him, and where he is, and most importantly, why Dad has never mentioned him. Weird.

Even weirder is that Uncle Ronald is not the only one who never died. Apparently, one Karenza Gwithyas, born in 1834, is still alive. So is Daisy Gwithyas, who was born about thirty years later. And Cecilia Gwithyas, born in 1766, and her brother Nathaniel, born in 1757, aren't dead either. Even one Jago Gwithyas, born in 1628, never died. He'd be pretty old now—about four centuries. Not very likely. There must be some other reason why those dates of death aren't on the family tree. Perhaps these people went missing, and no one knows when they died. Might that be what happened to Ronald?

Then it hits me. The one thing that is most wrong about this family tree. My sisters. Amethyst and Opal. They're not on it. There is my father's name, and my mother's, and together they have me. Only me. Peregrine Zircon Gwithyas, born on 31 October 2000. And no one else.

I sneak into my parents' bedroom. Dad is fast asleep. Mum has ordered me to let him rest, but this is too important. I need to know. I tap him on the arm.

"Dad?"

No response, so I tap harder. "Da-aaad!"

He produces a mighty snore. I grab his arm and shake it. "Dad! Wake up!"

He huffs and opens his eyes. "Whoa?"

"I need your help," I say.

He looks at me as if he's never seen anything more peculiar. Then he wakes up properly.

"Zircon," he says in a raspy voice. "What is it? Everything okay? Are you hurt?"

"No," I say, "but I've been studying the family tree, and it's wrong. Opal and Amethyst aren't on it."

Dad rubs his hand over his head and picks at his bandage. He looks puzzled about its presence, but leaves it as it is and says, "What are you babbling about boy? Of course they're on it."

"No, Dad, they aren't. Just look!"

I fold out the document and hold it in front of his face. He closes his eyes.

"Don't wave it about like that, you're making me dizzy. Give it to me!"

I hand him the family tree and he studies it. Then he points.

"There they are. Right under your name. Do you need new glasses again?"

I look. There's my name, with the Guardian symbol. There's Dad's name and Mum's name. No Opal and no Amethyst.

"They're not there!" I insist.

Dad taps his finger on an empty spot under my name. "Read, boy! Here they are. Perpetua Opal Gwithyas and Presencia Amethyst Gwithyas. Right here."

I look at the blank spot on the document. I may have poor vision, but if there'd been letters there I'd see them, even if I might not be able read them. There's definitely nothing. That bookcase must've done my father more harm than I thought. Perhaps I'd better not mention Uncle Ronald now.

"Right," I say while I take the family tree from him. "Never mind. Mum said you need your rest."

"A wise woman, your mother," mutters Dad, "but this is no time for idleness. I still need to tell you how to be a Guardian."

"Yeah," I agree. "You can do that another time."

"No!" says Dad. He rubs his head and groans. "You need

to defend it. The doorway, I mean. And for that, you need to know where it is."

I put my hand on his shoulder. "Take it easy, Dad."

He stops groaning and says, "Listen closely, boy. It all started when Graham was dying. His son was afraid. I don't think he cared much about his father, not any more, not after all the man had done, but Angus knew that if Graham died, his horrible creation would not die with him. It would continue to exist, free from the restraints of its creator's mind. That's when the witch stepped in."

I suppose he means Nanny. I wonder how she appeared in Dad's story all of a sudden, but then I consider that my father is suffering from a head injury so he's bound to be even less rational than usual.

"Sure," I say. "The witch. She came and made it all good, didn't she? So no need to worry. You can rest now."

Dad gives me an annoyed look. "Don't patronise me, boy. The witch lived at the manor. She was Angus' wife, and the mother of his children."

"Aha," I say, and I swallow back a sarcastic remark about five centuries old biddies in tower rooms and let my father continue his tale.

"Her sacrifice must have pained her more than anything," he says. "But she had little choice. She needed to protect the townsfolk, her children, and, even though she might not have suspected it at the time, all of humanity. With Graham gone another mind was needed to contain his insanity, and it had to be a mind with similar talents to Graham's. The only one available was her husband's. So the witch used her spells to anchor the Void and the doorway into Angus' mind, making him the first Guardian. With another spell she made sure that after Angus' death, the Void would be transferred to their eldest living child, and to their descendants for all eternity. And that is where the doorway is now. That is where the Void and all its horrors still reside."

He taps on his head. "In here, Zircon. Demons from the past. An insanity that isn't mine. A door between the two worlds. All fixed in the mind of the Guardian. And always, always they are trying to open that door, scraping at it with their claws, their teeth, their horns." His face gets flustered, and his hands twitch. "It hurts," he stammers. "It hurts so much, boy."

"You really need to rest, Dad," I say. "We can discuss this when you are better."

This time Dad doesn't tell me to stop patronising him. He just gives me a weak smile, lays his head on the pillow and mumbles, "Yes. I fear I do need to rest. Sorry about that, son. Don't worry. I'll be fit as a fiddle tomorrow, and we can talk about everything, and I'll tell you how to be a Guardian."

He is asleep before I'm out of the room.

It takes Dad quite a bit more than one day to get better. Fortunately, Nanny remains pretty much asleep the whole time, but it's frustrating that I can't ask my father anything. I told Mum about my visit and she gave me a good telling-off and won't let me get near their room anymore. Whatever. While she tends to Dad, I at least have the computer to myself. And that's good, because there is something I need to look up, and I prefer to do it in private.

So one morning, when my sisters are in their room and Mum is with Dad, I log onto Facebook for the first time in many weeks. In the search bar I type: '*Joanna Egwueke*'. Only one hit. I guess it's not a common name. I move my face nearer the screen to look at the profile picture. Joanna Egwueke is a dark-skinned girl with almond-shaped eyes and a big, bushy ponytail. Her face is a little wide and her teeth not all straight, but apart from that she is quite pretty.

Joanna's privacy settings are moderately strict. Apart from the basic information and her friends list I can't see anything. She has 634 friends at the moment, so she's not the choosy type. I send her a friend request. No personal message. I wouldn't know what to write. I'm just about to click Facebook away when a small icon flickers at me to inform me that my friend request has been accepted. When I click on Joanna's profile I feel queasy, but in a pleasant way.

Joanna lives in the town down the hill and attends the local college. Somehow that doesn't surprise me. She has not listed a relationship status. Pity. A small red icon pops up at the top of the page. I've received a private message. From Joanna.

"do i know you?" are my future wife's first words to me. She has used no capitals. Never mind; I'll lead by example.

My fingers tremble as I type: "mu name iS zircin fGithuss." Somehow I don't think that message will clarify the matter for her, so I correct it to: "My name is Zircon Gwithyas." Seems a bit dull. I want to write something that'll make her like me. Something touching, romantic, heart-warming. I type: "Your moist eyes are like pools of melted chocolate, and your teeth sparkle like snowflakes on an unwashed window."

And I click enter.

The reply is immediate, and not quite what I was hoping for. Something about bovine faecal matter. Apparently Joanna is not the romantic type.

I type back: "Sorry."

"i should kick u off rite now," messages Joanna, "but u get 1 chance. ru from that old manor up the hill?"

"Yes," I type, carefully avoiding using too many words. I wouldn't want to offend her again.

"k," she replies, "u can stay. just don't post on my wall. pm me if its urgent."

Urgent? I type back what kind of urgent she means, but she doesn't reply. Perhaps she's logged off. I wonder if I should send her another message. In my opinion my need for a girlfriend is pretty urgent. If Joanna's not romantic, I could always try a more direct approach. Of course that would never work if I had to say it to her in person. I'd never get the words out. But typing on the computer is a lot easier.

"You're really pretty," I type. "Shall we date? I can meet you down at the video library anytime this week."

That'll have to do. Enter.

As soon as I click Facebook away to log onto my discussion forum, Mum comes into the room and walks over to me.

"I heard Nanny's voice this morning, Zircon," she says. "We need to perform the ritual."

"It is definitely not my turn this time," I object.

Mum presses her lips together. "I'm sorry Zircon, but I'm afraid it's not a matter of turns any longer. We need a Guardian's powers. I'd do it myself if I could, but I am not a Guardian. I am only your father's shield. I can only do the ritual when he is awake so I can tap into his powers. That is not possible now, Zircon."

I twist on the chair so I can look Mum in the face. "If it's Dad's powers we need, then I can't do anything either."

Mum helplessly opens her hands. "You're the eldest," she says, "even if it is only by minutes. One day, you will be the Guardian. And judging from the way you performed the ritual the other day, you already have enough power to sustain Nanny for a bit longer. It's your responsibility now, Zircon. I wish it wasn't. I'm so sorry."

Yeah. I'm sorry too. Gutted would be a better word.

The climb up to the stairs is even gloomier than usual. Mum looks awful, as if she is constantly fighting back tears. She hasn't said a single word since we left the sitting room and when we reach the top of the stairs she opens the door to the tower room in silence.

Nanny is wriggling in her seat. She seems unusually restless. Her hands pluck at her ragged skirt while her feet, clad in the bright pink slippers that Mum bought her last month, shuffle over the floor. Her long greasy hair is so dishevelled that it hides her entire face from our view. Mum hands me the gems. I hesitate before putting them in place. By doing this I'm helping to keep alive the myth of the possessed woman in the tower, a myth I don't even believe in. What I ought to do is call in social services. I really should. It's hypocritical if I don't. And also, I really don't fancy having to do this daft ritual for who knows how long. I hate climbing up those stairs, I hate coming in this room. I hate seeing, or worse, feeling, Nanny.

"Hurry up, Zircon," says Mum, and her voice is so very tired. I start placing the gems. I don't want to stress Mum out even more. And, if I'm completely honest, I'm a little proud. Superstition or not, it's quite an honour to be responsible for the Guardian's task. I think Opal and Amethyst will be impressed when I tell them. And if that Joanna ever turns up . . . I stop myself. No daydreaming. No Joanna.

As I get ready to place the last artefact, the zircon, a chill runs down my spine, and suddenly I'm dizzy and nauseated. I compose myself and start to recite the enchantment. Mother joins in and we chant together, quietly and slowly. Just like always, but not really. This time the ritual affects me physically. Either that or I'm coming down with a bad flu. After every word I utter I feel a bit sicker, and when I'm at the fifth line a blinding pain rips through my head. I stagger and put my hands against the wall so I won't fall. I take a deep breath before blurting out the last two lines, and then I hear the sound of a door banging shut. The pain in my head immediately subsides, but I don't let go of the wall yet. I'm not confident that I can keep my balance. I shut my eyes and wait.

I had kind of expected Mum to start fussing over me, but she doesn't. When I look up to see why not, I see her standing a few feet away from me, staring at Nanny. Something's wrong. Mum's expression is even more tormented than when she came to call me earlier.

Nanny has raised her head and her thick strands of matted hair fall back so I can see her face. The sight almost makes me pass out. What I see is not the purple-tongued, flame-eyed monster I am accustomed to. What I see is a little old lady with a soft wrinkled face and a pair of unimaginably sad blue eyes, and she is gasping for air.

I cannot tell where the agonised moaning comes from. Is it Nanny? Is it Mum? Or even me? It doesn't matter. My mother rushes to Nanny, crying and stammering incoherent phrases. She pulls at the chains. With obvious effort Nanny raises her pale hand and rests it on Mum's head. "No, Louisa. Do not free me. It's too dangerous."

Mum whimpers and sinks to the floor. Her sobs echo through the room. Nanny turns her head to me.

"Come here, boy."

I shuffle towards her. It's an odd experience, for this time I am in full control of my legs.

"You released me," whispers Nanny. "The Koeg can no longer enter my body. Thank you for that. But you have a horrid task ahead of you, Zircon. I used up my last strength to help you lock the door, but it'll soon open again and I will not be here then." She raises a hand. I reluctantly take it. It's so small and so dry that I fear I will snap the fragile bones should I squeeze too hard. Nanny smiles.

"You are strong, Peregrine Zircon Gwithyas. Strong like Graham was. But do not make the same mistake! Remember: the magic of the hill is unstructured, a wild force of nature. To use it you need to control it, and for that you need the tools."

Nanny's eyes mist over. She blinks a few times and then she looks straight at me, and says, "The future is in your hands, but you cannot do it alone. Find your shield."

Before I can ask what she means her eyes roll back and her frail old body goes limp. Mum lets out a despairing wail. My head is throbbing as if someone is playing bongo on my brain.

Opal or Amethyst made Mum a cup of tea. Tea always helps her through difficult moments. I could use a cup myself, actually. My head really hurts.

"Could I . . ." I start, but Amethyst already hands me a

steaming mug. She also presses two paracetamol tablets in my hand.

"You look terrible," she says.

I'm surprised, but grateful. My little troll sisters. Who would ever expect them to be so considerate? They sit down next to each other and all three of us wait for Mum to speak. It takes a while, but then she sighs. It's a hopeless sound that seems to come from the deepest depths of her soul.

"Nanny is dead," she says, but of course we already knew that.

"I know that you all thought she was a monster," continues Mum. "Please don't remember her like that. She was a brave woman, who sacrificed herself to keep the rest of us safe. Over the last few years she has become weaker. Koeg kept attacking her, ravaging her body as well as her mind. We had to perform the ritual more and more often. It was only a matter of time before Nanny had to give up. I just hope she is at peace now."

Mum sniffs. Opal hands her a tissue, with which Mum dabs her eyes.

"There is so little I know," she says. "Your father knows more, but he… he just won't wake up. He has always kept so much from me. I suppose he wanted to protect me, in his own clumsy way. All I am certain off is my task. I am the shield, I am to protect the Guardian, your father. In that, I am failing. Your father… it's not just that concussion. He is very ill. His task as the Guardian is becoming too much for him to bear. And now that Nanny is no longer here to help . . ." Her lips tremble. She takes a sip of her tea.

"What was it exactly that Nanny did?" I ask. "And why was she so different just now? And what's the deal with the ritual and the gems? And what are those tools she was talking about?"

Mum looks confused. "So many questions, and I know so little." She gazes into her teacup as if the answers are hiding in there.

"Dad told me about the magic of the hill," I try. "Has it got to do with that?"

Mum tears her eyes away from her beverage.

"Yes," she says, 'the Gwithyas guards the insanity, and the witch's words, the spell, the enchantment, those are what shapes the magic. They keep the door closed."

"And the gems?"

"The gems are the structure. They link the witch and the Guardian with Graham's madness to contain it. Without the gems it would all fall apart. It was through the gems that I was able to perform the ritual, because when I focused on them they would show me into your father's mind, they would show me door to the Void. All I needed to do was shut it. For that, I used Nanny's words."

She brushes her hand over her forehead. "For your father it was different. The ritual affected him even when he was not performing it. The Koeg, Graham's monstrous creations, they are contained within Paul's mind. They are always there, always hurting him."

She turns to me. "It shall be like that for you, Zircon. Perhaps it already is, for this time it wasn't me who did the ritual. It obviously wasn't Paul either, he is too ill. Yet the door has never been shut so tightly before. Was it you Zircon? Did you do it?"

I hesitate. I didn't actually do anything. I only *heard* a door bang shut, but I didn't do it, and then Nanny died. I don't think I fancy this Guardian stuff. Perhaps simple inherited insanity isn't such a bad option after all.

"I only chanted," I say. "I didn't see a door."

Mum sighs. "I don't understand."

She stares at the wall. Opal, Amethyst and I sit quietly, waiting for her to tell us what will happen now, but Mum remains as silent as us. I start fidgeting with a loose thread from my jumper. I know how Mum hates it when I do that. She says it ruins perfectly good clothing. It works. She looks up.

"Stop that, Zircon!"

I stop. "What do we need to do to keep the doorway closed, Mum?" I ask.

Mum shakes her head. "I wish I knew."

Great. Nanny is dead, Dad is in a continuous daze, we have to shut a doorway that will otherwise lead evil monsters in to our house, my head is pounding as if someone is drilling holes into my frontal lobe, and Mum hasn't got the foggiest.

Luckily there are still my sisters.

"We can always ask the spirits," they say.

CHAPTER 5
Joanna

NEITHER MUM NOR I ARE QUITE UP TO SPIRITS, SO WE AGREE with Opal and Amethyst to try their idea tomorrow. Mum goes upstairs to tend to Dad. My sisters get their Ouija board out and place it on the side table, ready for use. I slouch on the sofa. I shouldn't really. I ought to do something, be pro-active, behave like a responsible Guardian-in-training.

What am I thinking? All this stuff about Guardians, magic, doorways and monsters from the Void is a delusion. I know that, and I should take charge now that we have a corpse in the tower. I should inform the authorities. All it would take is one call. I should pick up that phone right now. But I don't. What if it's all true? Then my one sensible call would flood the world with horrors beyond imagination.

My head throbs. The paracetamol isn't working. The headache affects my eyes, and even the diffuse light in the room irritates them. I take my glasses off to let my eyes rest. Only briefly. And then I'll do Guardian things, whatever they are, or call the police.

When I wake up I'm lying on the sofa under a duvet. I reach over to the side table where I have hopefully put my glasses. They are there, so I perch them on my nose and look around. I'm a tad disoriented. Sleeping during the day is not something

I normally do, certainly not on the sofa. At least my headache is almost gone. I wonder how long I dozed.

I look at the clock, an ancient thing with copper arms, as old as most things in this house but still in good working order. It's nearly four, which means I slept for over two hours.

I stand up and pick up the duvet. It's mine; the one with the Star Trek cover that Mum bought me for my tenth birthday. I suppose my sisters brought it here. I often told them not to enter my room with my explicit permission, but I think I'll let it go this time. It's kind of comforting to know that they did this for me. A bit worrying too, though. It makes me wonder if something is really wrong with me, something they don't tell me.

I stand still, my arms full of bedding, and I reflect on recent events. Nanny died. Did I kill her by doing the ritual? Or otherwise by failing to inform social services? Or did I imagine it all, and is she still alive, or did she never exist? I mean, it makes no sense. Perhaps because there is no sense to it, because I have no sense. What if it's not my parents and sisters who are delusional, but me, and they are simply taking loving care of their schizophrenic son and brother?

"Zircon?"

I twist on my heels to see who said that. It's only Amethyst.

"Are you feeling better?" she asks.

"Yes," I say. "I was just a bit tired. How's Mum?"

"She's with Dad. Opal is with them too."

That doesn't answer my question, but I feel too deflated to point that out. Amethyst takes the duvet from my arms.

"I'll take this back up," she says, and walks away. I ought to stop her and tidy up my own stuff, but I can't be bothered. My head is still not right, and I need peace and quiet. That, and Joanna.

I switch the computer on, wait impatiently for it to start up—has it always been this slow?—and then mouse to Facebook as fast as possible. I have a message. From Joanna. I almost hyperventilate with anticipation when I open it, but the words are not quite what I was hoping for.

"stop stalking me"

I read it again. It still says, quite undeniably: "stop stalking me"

I stare at the screen, not sure what to think. Stalkers are creepy, desperate, sex-obsessed psychos. I'll admit to being desperate, but I doubt that I'm more sex-obsessed than the average sixteen-year-old male, and I've never seen myself as creepy. My fingers hover over the keyboard. What should I type now? Should I type anything at all?

Then I see the other message. Also from Joanna. Of course it is, there's no one else on my friends list. The message is longer than the first, but not particularly more friendly.

"ur a freak. the only reason i did not delete u is cuz ur from the manor. get off my back. only pm me if its urgent and it has to do with the guardian, get that? now leave me alone."

I let my hands drop so they dangle limply at my sides. Joanna thinks I'm a freak. Joanna knows about the Guardian. Joanna wants me to leave her alone. Joanna wants me to contact her when it's urgent. I stare at the screen. I should type a message back, apologise, make her like me a little better. Certainly if it's true that she and I are supposed to get married.

I put my fingers on the keyboard, but can't think of anything to type, and anyway, I don't expect that Joanna really wants another message from me anyway. Bwah. If this is what romance is like I don't want it. I log out, switch the computer off and get up. Amethyst is sitting on a cushion on the floor, browsing a booklet about advanced witchcraft. I didn't hear her come back. She looks up when I let myself fall onto the sofa.

"Everything okay?"

"Yeah," I mutter, and I poke at my fingernails. They need cutting.

"Mum is coming down," says Amethyst. "With Opal. Mum thinks we ought to talk to the spirits now."

Now? I thought she wanted to wait until tomorrow. I hope it

doesn't mean that Dad is getting worse. When my mother enters the room, her face is pale and without expression. She heads straight for the Ouija board and kneels down.

"You three do it," she says. "I shall watch."

So once again we are on the ragged carpet in the sitting room with our fingers on the Ouija cursor. Opal, Amethyst and me. I feel a bit weird. I used to consider this practice all a whole load of bogus, only a silly fantasy of two silly girls, but I'm not so sure now. After all that has happened spirits might just as well be real. No, I shouldn't think such things. Keep your wits, Zircon Gwithyas.

Amethyst prods my arm and says, "Ask a question."

"Why me?" I ask. "I know nothing of Ouija! You two are forever fiddling with it, not me!"

"We've asked all our questions. It's your turn," insists Amethyst.

Opal adds, "The spirits have nothing to say to us two anymore."

I hesitate only briefly before giving in. I know my sisters. If they really want something, they back each other up and no one can change their minds. So I touch the cursor and ask, "What should we do about the doorway, and Nanny, and everything else?"

Nothing happens. The cursor just sits there.

"I think your spirits are having their supper," I joke.

Supper. I'm getting hungry. It's getting late. A huge portion of chips with salt and vinegar would go down just fine right now.

"Ask again," urges Opal. "And stop thinking about food, you greedy pig."

I raise my eyebrows at my sister. "So you can mind-read as well now, can you?" I ask.

"No," says Opal. "You were licking your lips. Besides, you're always thinking about food."

She is exaggerating of course. I have been eating quite a lot lately, but, as Dad says, a growing boy needs his calories.

"Ask!" nags Amethyst.

I push the chips from my thoughts, slide my fingers over the cursor and say, "Ohh, sweet clever spirits, please tell us what we should do to get our house back in order, and how we keep the monsters out."

Nothing happens.

"Told you," I say to Opal and Amethyst, but then something trembles under my fingers. The Ouija cursor is moving after all. Slowly, uncertainly, but it is moving all right. Seeking out letters on the board. First the 'G'. Next, the letter 'E', and after that it moves a little bit faster. As if it's learning how to do it. One by one the letters are chosen. After G-E follow T-J-O-A-N-N-A.

"G.E. Tjoanna?" muses Amethyst.

"Get Joanna," I whisper.

"Who's Joanna?" asks Opal.

Seems I have some potentially embarrassing explaining to do.

We gather around the computer. Me on the chair, Mum standing behind me, and Amethyst and Opal to my left and right. I didn't want them to watch. I didn't even want to tell them that I know who Joanna is, and that I have a way of contacting her. I seriously considered just keeping my mouth shut, but then there was Mum's exasperated face, and my sisters' prying eyes, and my own desire to meet my appointed spouse in person.

I didn't tell Mum and the girls everything. I didn't tell them that Joanna is down on the family tree as my wife. Nor did I tell them that she considers me a freak and a stalker. In fact, all I said that I know her from Facebook, and that she lives in town, and that she knows about the Guardian, and she said to contact her if it's urgent.

"Few things are more urgent than a direct request from the spirits," Opal said to that. I just hope Joanna agrees with her.

I log on to Facebook. Now to contact Joanna. Not as

straightforward as it seems. The private messages that she and I exchanged are still in my message box, and I definitely do not want my mother and sisters to read them. But Joanna doesn't want me to post on her wall.

"I need some privacy," I say.

"Not on the internet you don't," says my mother. "You are still a minor, Zircon."

I hate it when she suddenly becomes all sensible. I decide it's best to not argue, and I go to Joanna's wall. I hope she hasn't blocked me from posting. I point at her profile pic.

"T-this is her," I stammer, and my cheeks get warm.

Amethyst sniggers, and Opal says, "I think Zircon likes her."

"I barely know her!"

My traitorous voice goes just a little too high. Better change the subject.

"Now what do I type?" I ask.

"Tell her the spirits are calling for her," says Amethyst.

"Tell her the witch is dead," says Mum.

"Tell her the Koeg are coming," says Opal.

I should've known better than ask my family for advice. I don't even want to contemplate how any of these messages would come across to Joanna's friends, now 637, who can all see her wall as clearly as I can. So I type, "We're in trouble. You said to contact you. Please come."

That'll have to do. Enter.

I swivel round with my office chair.

"She might not be on now," I explain. "So we have to wait."

"She's on," says Opal, pointing at the screen. Joanna has reacted to my message.

"see u in 20 minutes."

"That's fast," says Mum. "You'd think she was expecting this."

"A well-drilled shield," comments Amethyst.

"Just what we need," agrees Opal.

I barely hear them. My heart is beating too loudly. Twenty minutes. My love life will commence in twenty minutes. I need to cut my nails. Comb my hair. Change clothes. And it wouldn't harm to clean my teeth as well. I log out and click Facebook away. I mumble something about needing to do stuff and rush to the bathroom.

When I return fifteen minutes later, tidily dressed, my mouth smelling of spearmint, my hair arranged in a state that vaguely resembles order, and my nails clean and short, Mum and the girls are sitting next to each other on the sofa. They're trying to act as if they're doing only that—sitting—but from their plank-straight backs and slightly tilted heads I can tell that they're in fact nervously listening for that knock on the door.

We don't get many visitors. In fact, we don't get any, ever. The midwife who helped deliver my sisters and me was probably the last one. Ordinary people don't like to mingle with lunatics in a haunted house on a cursed hill.

"Who will open the door?" asks Opal.

"Me of course!" I say.

"I think it'd be better if we did it," says Amethyst. "You might faint when you see her."

I squint at her, trying to keep my cool. "I'll have to open it. If you did it, it might well be Joanna who faints!"

"Zircon!" says Mum reproachfully. "Don't talk to your sister like that! It is probably best if I go."

Opal and Amethyst wobble-shake their big heads. "She'd be more at ease with girls her own age."

"Don't be ridiculous," I say. "I'm the one who messaged her, so I ought to . . ."

Opal sticks her hand up. "Hush!"

I almost get angry with her for interrupting me, but then I hear it too. Knocking. Loud, persistent knocking. On the front door. It is a sound alien to us. We look at each other. Mum, Opal, Amethyst and me. For a second, all remains still. Then there is another knock, three even. *Knock knock knock!*

I soar out of the room while Mum stumbles from her seat

and my sisters slowly rise. They're way behind me when I dash through the corridor.

Our front door is massive and made of solid wood. Dad once told me it was wood from a very rare tree that only grows in the Norwegian mountains. I'm not sure I believe that. To me it looks like local oak. It's elaborately decorated with crudely carved images of monsters. This door used to scare the pants off me when I was younger. I have outgrown that fear, but I'm getting pretty irritated when the rusty old lock won't open. I want this door open immediately so I can be the first to speak to Joanna.

I fidget feverishly with the key while Mum's regular footsteps echo through the corridor. The lock clicks. The door creaks, squeaks and grunts when I open it to reveal our first visitor in over sixteen years.

The outside light is so bright that I can only see the outline of our guest. She is about as tall as I am and has lots of hair. When my eyes have adapted to the light I see that she's wearing heavy walking boots, jeans and a bright pink t-shirt. She is also holding a massive double-edged sword with which she prods my nose-tip.

"This better be a real emergency," she says. "If I find out that you lured me here 'cause you're randy I'll have you arrested for stalking."

To say that I am astonished would be an understatement. It's not because she is carrying a lethal weapon and threatens me with it, though I admit that that's unsettling, but what shocks me most are her eyes. So large, shiny, dark and delicately shaped. And her skin, so warm brown, almost glowing with radiant health. And her mouth, with its smooth, full lips, and perfectly imperfect white teeth. All that framed by a halo of dark brown, soft, frizzy hair.

As my mother's footsteps become louder Joanna lowers her sword. The footsteps stop just behind me.

"Don't stand there gazing at her!" snaps my mother before she pushes me out of the way.

"Joanna?" she says in a completely different tone of voice.

"Thank you so much for coming so quickly. Come in, do come in immediately, it's nippy outside! Would you like a cup of tea?"

"Oh, yes please, thank you ever so much," replies Joanna with a voice like cheering songbirds and the rustling of leaves in a soft summer wind.

If she's in the least surprised that my mother knows her name she doesn't show it. As she walks past me I catch a whiff of jasmine. I forget to move. I gawk at Joanna while she, my mother and my sisters walk through the corridor.

"Don't forget to shut the door, darling!" calls my mother as she steps into the sitting room. Joanna follows her, and only once the last of her brown curls has disappeared from my view do I come to my senses. I pull the door to, which is not as easy as it sounds because the thing is ridiculously heavy, and then I follow the womenfolk into the room.

My mother is making tea in the kitchen. Joanna, Opal, Amethyst and I sit quietly in our murky front room. Joanna has picked the chair near the table, the one with the once-green cover and fraying golden tassels. She sits very straight, clearly not relaxed, her hand firmly clenching her sword's hilt. She keeps glancing apprehensively at my sisters. Not surprising. The way they sit there, on the darkest chair in the darkest corner of the room, hunched closely together, they look like a two-headed, pale grey goblin skeleton.

I clear my throat. All three, my sisters as well as Joanna, look at me. My cheeks feel suspiciously hot when I say in my most masculine voice, "May I welcome you to our humble abode?"

Joanna raises her eyebrows. "Abode?" she repeats with a smirk. "What era are you from?"

Hm. Actually those dark almond eyes of hers are a little bit on the wonky side, if you look closely.

"I'm just trying to be polite," I say.

Joanna snorts. "Polite. I'm surprised you even know the word. Or did you really think it's 'polite' to harass a girl on Facebook?"

I cringe. My sisters glare at me inquisitively.

"I didn't mean to upset you," I mutter. "I'm sorry."

"You're a bit slow, aren't you?" says Joanna. "Those coke-bottles on your nose must be blurring your brain as well as your eyes. I'm not upset. I'm grossed out."

There seems to be a rather unpleasant hoarse quality to her voice. Odd that I didn't pick that up at first. I bite my lip and look down. None of us says anything else. I study the layout of the floorboards until my mother enters the room, carrying a huge tray with a teapot, cups, and a large plate of biscuits. I didn't even know we had biscuits in the house.

"Oh, that looks absolutely lovely, Mrs Gwithyas!" chirps Joanna.

Mum smiles widely and says, "It's nothing, Joanna. This is just my way to welcome you to our humble abode."

Joanna doesn't even wince when she replies, "Thank you, Mrs Gwithyas. It is my honour."

I wait until I have my tea before I look at her again, because I figure that it's less conspicuous to observe the state of affairs from behind the brim of my cup.

Joanna munches her way through an impressive amount of biscuits. Mum is still smiling. Opal and Amethyst lurk in their dark corner, ogling Joanna. Four beady eyes peeking at you from those pale blots of faces is enough to make anyone nervous, and I can tell that in spite of her polite conversation with Mum, Joanna is getting more edgy by the minute. I'll be damned if I care. Stupid expression. I am damned anyway. My head hurts, too. I lean back in the huge brown chair and sigh. This will be a lot less pleasant than I had hoped.

Mum says, "Zircon told us you know about the Guardian."

"Ah, yes," says Joanna. She takes her last sip of tea, puts the cup on the table, and says, "I do know about the Guardian. I have always known."

And then she tells us about herself. She's an orphan, and she was brought up by her uncle.

"His name is Rupert Grenville," she says. "He is a direct descendant of the witch."

She takes a bite from another biscuit, her ninth if I counted correctly, and says to my mother, "These are lovely. Did you bake them yourself?"

My mother nods contentedly. She doesn't often get compliments about her cooking. Joanna shoves the rest of the biscuit into her mouth, swallows, and continues her tale.

"My uncle said that I have a very important destiny, that I am a magical warrior. He taught me how to fight with a sword, because modern weapons like guns and stuff would be useless against the dangers—Uncle called them the Koeg—that lurk here, in this manor. My uncle also told me that the Guardian lives in the manor, and that he is a brave and powerful man who keeps the Koeg at bay even though he suffers horribly, and that I'm his protector, his shield."

My mother frowns. "Suffers horribly? Did your uncle say how horribly?"

"No," says Joanna. "Anyway, if I do my job right, his suffering shouldn't be too great."

"Yes," says Mum. "Let's hope so." She takes a deep breath, smiles at Joanna once more and says, "Either way, we are very grateful that you came, Joanna. And on such short notice."

"Not that short," says Joanna. "I've been warned to expect a call, and that was over a week ago."

"Warned?" Mum looks surprised. "How? By whom?"

"I got a letter," says Joanna, "Personal delivery, too. Stuck to my bedroom window with sellotape. It was signed Paul Gwithyas."

All colour drains from my mother's face. "Paul Gwithyas?" she whispers. "Paul? No. He can't have!"

I put my hand on Mum's arm. "It must've been a forged signature, Mum."

I turn to Joanna. "Paul is my father," I explain. "He is the Guardian. At the moment he's in bed with a concussion. The thing is, he never leaves the house, he says he always needs to be here to guard the doorway, and I'm sure he didn't neglect his task only to stick a note to special little Joanna's bedroom window."

Joanna gives me an aggrieved look.

"Well, I didn't make it up! There was a letter! You don't honestly think your neurotic Facebook posts would be enough to get me to visit a bunch of misshapen lunatics in a smelly old dump of . . ."

She swallows her last words and looks anxiously at my mother. But Mum is deep in thought and hasn't heard a word of Joanna's outburst.

"Perhaps," she mumbles. "Perhaps he knew." She blinks and then turns to Joanna, smiling. "Sorry, I was miles away. What did you say, darling?"

Joanna's velvety cheeks get a tad darker, and I can't help but feel good at her embarrassment, but before I get the chance to make fun of her, Opal's sharp voice pinches from the dark corner.

"What did the note say?" she asks, and Joanna seizes the opportunity to change the subject.

"The letter said I had to be prepared, it said that the Guardian would need me sooner than anticipated."

"That's all?" I say sarcastically. "And for that, you run up the hill to this smelly old dump with its misshapen lunatics of inhabitants? How heroic of you."

Mum looks shocked. "Zircon!" she says reproachfully, but she doesn't give me a lecture. She sighs, messes up my hair and stands up.

"I'll go check on your father," she says before leaving the room.

Opal, Amethyst and I are left in the room with Joanna. There's an awkward silence. I desperately want to end it, but don't know how. What do I say? I open my mouth, and shut it again just as quickly. I wouldn't know how to start. I guess growing up as a recluse isn't good for one's social skills. It's Joanna who eventually breaks the silence.

"So, any chance that I'll get to speak to your father?"

"He's ill," says Amethyst.

"He needs his rest," confirms Opal.

"Oh," says Joanna a bit taken aback. "But I really should. I mean, I'm here to help, right? To assist the Guardian. So I need to at least speak to him."

"Not now," says Amethyst. She stands up and nods at Joanna. "I'll show you the guest room. Maybe our father will feel better tomorrow."

"Okay," agrees Joanna, and she gets up, turns to me and clears her throat.

"I'm sorry that I was so crabby before," she says. "I mean, I still think you shouldn't have bugged me on Facebook, and you're weird, but I guess that with living here and all, that isn't really your fault. And I was nervous. I tend to do that, you know, when I get nervous. Nag at people I mean."

It takes me a few seconds to get my vocals going.

"It's okay," I stammer, and she smiles. I smile back and decide that the wonkiness of her eyes must have been a trick of the light, as right now they simply look gorgeously almond-shaped. Joanna follows my sister out of the room. Even her back is enchanting.

CHAPTER 6
Dreams

THOUGHT OR SPEECH, THE DIFFERENCE IS TRIVIAL. IMAGES OR imagination, ideas or reality . . . is there a distinction at all? They flutter, vibrate, barely there yet undeniably present. They're calling me, or are they? A man stands there, looking at me. He looks like my father.

"Zircon," he says, and he even sounds like my father. Our eyes meet. I avert mine. It hurts. Such emptiness, such an incomprehensible void. "I am your uncle, Zircon."

"Uncle Ronald?"

He smiles. "You read about me, didn't you?"

How does he know that?

"I've been watching you," he says. "I am here to help. To give guidance, rather, for you don't need help. You are strong, Zircon. You don't need the witch, or your father, or even me. The only one you need is the creator of the Void. You need Graham Gwithyas."

Well, that's a fat lot of help. Graham Gwithyas has been dead for centuries. I didn't think I had said this out loud, but I must have, because my uncle nods in agreement, and says, "Graham has died, but he has not passed. The witch trapped him, she trapped his mind and his powers, and she used them to keep the door shut. She could access him and his creation through the link. Do you know about the link? It's an enchanted part of the planet Earth. A part that you have in your possession."

He's rambling. I think I'd know it if I were carrying a lump of possessed mud around with me. My uncle raises his upper lip, exposing his teeth like an angry dog, and snarls, "Don't be an idiot."

I pull my duvet up higher. He's moody, my uncle. When he detects my unease his expression softens.

"I apologise," he says. "I'm sure you understand. It is the pressure I am under. Of course, that is no excuse to lose my temper."

He smiles again. He looks a lot like my father when he smiles. I relax.

"You have it," Uncle Ronald insists. "The gem."

Gem?

"Yes," says Uncle Ronald. "The zircon from the ritual. Don't you remember? You took it with you when the witch died. The stone is the link. Through it, you can enter Graham's mind. Where is it?"

And then I remember. That last ritual . . . I never placed the zircon on the floor. I must've put it in my pocket instead. In the pocket of my jeans, to be exact. The same jeans that are now lying in a messy heap next to my bed. I reach down and pull the trousers towards me.

"No need to get dressed," remarks my uncle.

I stick my hand in the back pocket and pull out the gem. It shimmers in my hand. I show it to Uncle Ronald. "Is this what you mean?"

He produces a constrained whimper. "Yes!" he gasps. "Yes! With this gem there will be no limits to what we can do. Give it to me, Zircon. I'll keep it safe."

I look at the zircon in my hand. Its orange glow makes my fingers appear even more spindly and knobbly than usual, but apart from that the gem is unremarkable.

"It's just a stone, nothing more," I say.

"Give!" insists my uncle. His stretched-out hand is trembling. I hesitate. My uncle is a tad too excited. I'm not so certain that he is in the right state of mind to be in control of potential great powers.

"No," I say. "I reckon it's better if I hang onto this for the moment."

Ronald narrows his eyes and raises his lip. I glimpse the stained yellow of his teeth. His mouth opens. Will he speak? His mouth continues to open. Wider and wider, so the lips stretch out over his nose and chin, then over his eyes, until his entire head tears apart into a quivering mass of soggy flesh. I pull my hand back, clutching the zircon, and watch in horror as my uncle's skin starts to melt, dripping from his flesh like hot wax from a candle. He is still attempting to speak. The words from his dissolving mouth are warped and I can only just make out my own name.

"Zircon! Zircon!"

I struggle to get up, but I slip in my own sweat, or his melted skin, and then there is laughter. Uncle Ronald, now nothing but a smouldering skinless corpse, collapses in a silent heap as the laughter grows louder, so loud that I fear my eardrums will rip. I tear myself from my bedsheets and leap up, ready to run. To my surprise my eyes flick open. I didn't even know they'd been shut. The laughter stops and there is only darkness. I sink down until I am kneeling on my mattress. I press my duvet close against my chest and wait until I stop hyperventilating before lying down again. It was a dream. Only a dream. I'm so cold that I can barely bend my fingers enough to pull the duvet back over me. I shut my eyes but I don't sleep any more.

We're all sitting around the kitchen table, having our breakfast. Porridge for Joanna, Mum and me. Opal and Amethyst nibble on a dry cracker each. Apparently they have even less appetite than usual. Not that I feel like eating a lot. I've stirred my porridge seven times now, and I've not eaten a single spoonful. I'm just not hungry. Or perhaps I'm too tired to eat. I can't have had more than three hours sleep last night. I'm not sure if I should tell Mum, or my sisters, or even Joanna about my dream. If it was a dream at all. It was so vivid. And this morning . . . I touch my trouser pocket. It's still there, my gem, the orange zircon. I found it on the carpet when I got up. It must've dropped it when I slipped, because it was lying in the middle of a slightly sticky stain. The remnants of melted skin? I push my bowl away. Mum eyes me with obvious concern.

"Aren't you hungry, Zircon? And the girls aren't eating either! Oh dear, I hope there isn't a bug going round!"

A bug. Good old Mum, once again thoroughly in denial.

Joanna has eaten a substantial amount, but she too seems pre-occupied. She has said very little.

"Did you sleep well?" I ask her, for lack of anything better to say.

She gazes in my general direction, clearly elsewhere with her thoughts. Then she flutters her eyelashes. Long, dark, curly eyelashes that land on her suede cheeks like falling cherry blossom petals on soft spring grass. I cringe at my own tacky clichés; at least I didn't say it out loud. Joanna doesn't reply and continues to absent-mindedly do the petal-on-grass thing, so I repeat my question.

"Did you sleep well, Joanna?"

"Sleep . . ." she echoes. "No, no. I didn't sleep too well." She looks at Mum apologetically. "It is a lovely room, Mrs Gwithyas, and a very comfortable bed. It's just that I had some strange dreams."

My sisters look up from their barely-touched crackers.

"Dreams carry meaning," says Opal.

"Dreams tell the truth," adds Amethyst.

I sure hope she's wrong there.

"What did you dream?" I ask Joanna.

She shrugs. "It didn't seem like a dream. There were spiders. Orange spiders, three of them. But later there were only two, and a woman who let them run up and down her arms. She looked at me, and her eyes . . ." Joanna shivers. "Old, old eyes they were, and so horribly sad that I couldn't bear to look at them. Then she said my name. She called me the warrior. She said that I was strong, and I would have to be. She said the Guardian is not well, and that he can't do it alone. He is in danger and he needs me. Then she got up and walked away. The spiders followed her, and I was alone in the dark."

Hm. It seems Joanna got the better deal, dreamwise. Opal and Amethyst bobble-nod.

"We like spiders," they say. "Especially orange ones."

"I think I really need to speak to the Guardian," says Joanna. "Could I please see your husband, Mrs. Gwithyas?"

"He wasn't very well this morning," says Mum.

"I'm his shield," argues Joanna. "He needs me."

My mother presses her lips together and shakes her head. "No."

Then she gets up and asks us if we want some hot chocolate. We don't.

The day passes uneventfully. Mum spends most of her time looking after Dad. Opal and Amethyst whisper to each other and I lounge on the sofa. I don't feel well. That dream really got to me. Joanna fiddles with her sword and paces about the room. She looks from the girls to me and back, and eventually decides to go for me.

"Are you always this lazy?" she asks.

"No," I say. "There's just nothing to do."

"I thought there was a world to save?"

"Yeah, well, when you find out how, tell me," I reply.

"Oh, I will find out," she says. "I just think that you could put in some effort too. Don't you have any books in this house that we can read? Or some other sort of information?"

"I have a headache," I say. "But if you are really desperate to waste your time, my father's office is down the corridor, first door to the left. You can't miss it. All the furniture is in shatters."

Joanna squints at me, and when I say nothing else she says, "Very well. I'll go. You just stay here, lying around like a bag of mouldy bread."

She turns on her heels and leaves the room. I shut my eyes. I really have a headache, and it's a bad one too. Mum was right after all. I'm definitely coming down with something.

"Zircon?"

Opal's voice is quiet, yet insistent.

"What?" I ask, without opening my eyes.

"Do you think it's a good idea to let her into Dad's office on her own?"

"What's the harm?"

I say that, but I know very well what my sister means. Of course it's not a good idea, if only because of Dad's right to privacy. He hasn't even met Joanna. Even more importantly, I have no idea what kind of documents Dad keeps in his office. I only ever looked in the secret compartment, but there could be anything; personal stuff, dangerous stuff, possibly even illegal stuff. Perhaps medical evidence of serious inherited mental disorders, or subpoenas to call my parents to court for the abuse of Nanny. Of course there's a good chance that there is nothing like that, but can I take the risk?

The scene from the mentally ill in 'One Flew over the Cuckoo's Nest' pops up again, and I open my eyes. I snarl accusingly at Opal, as if she was the one who's been scaring me with paranoid ideas, "Fine, fine! I'll go after her already."

I sit up and wince as a sharp ache rips through my head. I stay on the sofa with my head in my hands until the pain subsides, and when I look up Opal is staring at me. If her facial muscles were better developed she'd look worried.

"Are you all right?" she asks.

I get up from the sofa and run my fingers through my hair. "I'm fine," I say. "Just a bit of a headache."

I feel Opal's eyes in my back while I walk out of the room. I don't think she believed me. Doesn't matter. I need to get to the office. I am suddenly in a hurry. How could I be so stupid? The thought of someone, a virtual stranger, rummaging in my father's papers without any supervision makes me sick. Or perhaps I was sick already, because I'm finding it unusually hard to walk. I stagger through the corridor to the office door.

Joanna is sitting cross-legged in the mess, a neat pile of papers next to her. I stop in the doorway and glance nervously at the A4 in her hands.

"What's that?" I ask. "What are you reading? You shouldn't just browse through other people's personal documents, you know."

She raises her eyebrows. "I quite clearly recall you telling me to do exactly that."

"Yes, but…" I say, and as I try to come in further I trip over a piece of wood and nearly fall. Joanna hastily moves out of the way.

"Watch out!"

"Sorry," I huff, once I have found my balance again. "Anyway, about those documents. I didn't mean for you to read them. I wasn't thinking clearly and… ehm . . ." My mind goes blank and I rub my achy forehead.

"And nothing, apparently," remarks Joanna. "You're too late anyway. I've already found some fascinating stuff."

She gestures at the pile next to her. My legs are so wobbly that I think I may fall over, so I sit down on a cracked plank opposite Joanna and place my head on my knees.

"Are you okay?" Joanna asks in the same annoying concerned tone of voice as my sister.

"Yes," I say, and I sit up straight. "So what did you find then?" As if I really want to know.

"Weird stuff," she says. "But first there's something else, something I haven't been able to figure out, and would really like to know. What happened to this office?"

"Woodworm," I say.

"Woodworm," she repeats. "I see. Right."

"What did you find out?" I ask again.

Joanna holds up a small booklet. I say booklet, but it's really nothing but a bunch of papers tied together with a string of thread.

"This speaks of a doorway that leads to another place," says Joanna. "Your ancestors don't seem to agree what that place is. Some call it Hell, others say it is a different realm, yet others call it the Void, and one reckons it's Belgium."

"Yeah," I say, relieved that she doesn't mention mental illness or social services. "I knew that. About the doorway I mean. Not about my loopy ancestor who thinks it leads to Belgium. It's what we guard, isn't it? The doorway."

"We?" repeats Joanna. "I thought only your father is the Guardian?"

"He is," I say. "But when he is… gone… I'll be the Guardian."

Joanna blinks. "You?"

"Apparently. If you believe all that rubbish about monsters and doorways and rituals."

"Do you mean that you don't believe it?"

I shrug. "Not really. I mean, it all seems a bit far-fetched, doesn't it?"

Joanna looks at me as if I'm a pile of dog droppings and asks, "Do you at least know where that doorway is? I'd like to see it. Can you show it to me?"

"No," I say. "I can't, because it doesn't exist. And anyway, according to the legend it's not really a physical doorway. It's more like a spiritual portal, and from what I gathered, it should be in here."

I tap on my head. Joanna is silent for a while.

"Okay," she eventually says slowly. "Maybe I should ask something else. These papers also talk about a witch. Any idea who that is?"

"Yeah," I say, trying to ignore the repeated sharp pangs behind my eyes. "She's my Nan. Was. She wasn't really my Nan actually. And she's dead. She died a few days ago."

"Died?"

"She'd been getting weaker," I explain. "And the last ritual was too much. Says my Mum. I reckon Nanny just had a heart attack."

"You don't seem to be too bothered about that," remarks Joanna.

"I am!" I say. "But she was really old, and she's probably better off dead. And I'm glad that I don't have to climb up those tower stairs twice a week any longer."

"Tower? Your Nanny was in a tower? The thin tower in your garden? And you did rituals in there?" She puckers her lips and puts her finger to them. "I think I'd like to see that tower," she says.

Figures. A gloomy tower is more to her liking than the mind of a ginger geek. She hops up from the office floor in a nauseating display of physical vigour.

"Show me," she orders.

Hah. No way I'm clambering up all those steps.

"Another time," I say while I force myself back on my feet. My head is pounding, and I'm seeing stars. I point at Joanna. "You have to leave this office. Now."

I know I'm being rude, but I can't think straight. I mutter something about my games console and scurry past Joanna to get to my bedroom.

When I wake up the pain is gone. I vaguely recall vomiting into the toilet bowl before hauling myself into bed, and the taste of sour dairy products in my mouth confirms that recollection. I'm still shaky, and my legs feel unreliable as I make my way to the bathroom to clean my teeth.

When I'm all minty again, I go downstairs to the sitting room. My sisters are there, rummaging through their box of occult toys, and Joanna is reading a book. All three look up when I enter, but only Joanna speaks.

"Enjoyed your animated pixels?" she asks.

For a moment I can't understand what she's talking about, but then I remember. I told her I'd be at my games console.

"Yeah," I say, and she snorts.

"You are quite something, aren't you? Your father is ill, your Nan died, the world is gonna be swarmed with bloodthirsty demons and you go beat your high score on superspaceships or whatever."

"I don't play superspaceships," I argue, but she's already got her nose back in her book. I want to say something witty, but nothing comes to mind and I turn to my sisters instead.

"What are you doing?"

"Nothing in particular," says Opal. "Would you like some hot chocolate?"

I blink. "Would I want what?"

"Hot chocolate," repeats Opal. "It'd do you good."

Amethyst gets up. "I'll make it for you."

My mouth falls open when Amethyst actually makes her way to the kitchen.

"Spoiled little prince," mumbles Joanna from behind her book.

CHAPTER 7
Undesirable

Opal and Amethyst are creepily nice to me and Joanna clearly doesn't approve. She rolls her eyes when Amethyst hands me the hot chocolate. I sit down on the sofa and drink. There's lots of sugar in it, and it's hot and foamy. With every sip I feel less shaky.

"Thanks," I say. I can't understand why my sisters are being so uncharacteristically kind, but I'm glad that they are. Amethyst takes my cup back to the kitchen, while Opal takes the occult box back to their bedroom. Joanna leans over to me.

"Are you finished?" she asks. "Perhaps then your highness could do me the honour of showing me that tower?"

I'd really rather not. The idea of climbing up all those stairs and going into Nanny's room doesn't remotely appeal to me, but I don't want to disgruntle Joanna even more.

"All right," I say. "It's quite a climb though."

Joanna follows me out of the house and into the tower. The climb up the stairs seems longer than usual, and when we are about two thirds up I'm out of breath and light-headed. My legs are trembling. I clutch the railing.

"Maybe," I wheeze, "h-have a little rest, okay?"

Without waiting for a response I sink down on a step. I expect

Joanna to make a snappy remark, but she doesn't. She just waits silently while I'm catching my breath. I'm embarrassed. I want to tell her that I'm not usually this flimsy, that I'm sick, and that I don't want to go the tower room, and that there is no doorway there anyway, but I don't think she'd be interested. So I just sit until I'm sort of able to drag myself up the last part of the stairs.

The door is open. Was it open when Mum and I left? And hell, what happened to Nanny's body? I don't recall Mum even mentioning it. Is it still there, chained to the chair, slowly decomposing? Now what wouldn't make a good impression on Joanna. I try to come up with a reason to go back without entering the room, but Joanna wriggles past me through the door opening and I have no choice but to follow her.

To my surprise and relief there is no Nanny. No body, no chains, not even the chair is there any longer. Just the walls, the floor and the pentagram. It's cold, though, colder than it's ever been in here. I shiver. Joanna doesn't seem bothered by the low temperature. She glances around curiously.

"So where is that doorway?"

"I told you," I say. "In my mind. Or rather, in my father's mind, because he's the Guardian. Or ratherder even, in my ancestors' minds if it's all a fairy tale. Which is what I believe anyway. There is no doorway. I don't believe it exists. There certainly are no doorways here in this room other than the one we just came through, and . . ."

"Stop rambling," says Joanna. "And for the record; there's no such word as ratherder."

She turns her back to me and starts to search the room, touching and prodding the walls as if she expects some secret entrance to spring open. She must've read too many mystery novels.

I too look around in case there is a forgotten candlestick somewhere, or, more gruesomely, some detached piece of Nanny. I don't find any of those things, but I do find something else. Tiny, sparkly shards. Black ones, and purple, green and red ones.

The gems. They must have shattered during that last ritual. All except the zircon. I pick up the shards, and while I am doing that Joanna asks, "Are you retarded?"

"What?" I ask. "No. Of course not!"

"You sure? No learning disabilities? Did you ever take an IQ test?"

"I did one online," I say. "And for your information, I scored pretty high."

"Really?" sneers Joanna. "So if you're so clever, then what is your excuse?"

"Excuse?"

"Yes. For being so completely useless."

I cringe. As usual I fail to come up with a witty reply, so I just continue to search the floor for rogue gem shards. Joanna snorts, and when I look up she is running her finger over the wall again, and ignoring me. I continue to look at her. She's so pretty. People might reckon I can't possibly judge female beauty since the only women I ever get close too are my Mum, who doesn't really count, my troll sisters and Ms. Chen who I never get to observe properly because I usually don't have my glasses on for long enough when I'm there.

But those people would be wrong. I've been to town, and I watch telly. So I know what girls look like. Now Joanna doesn't actually look like those girls on TV. She's too muscular, and the skin on her face is a little blotchy. Still, she's beautiful. And she is the only real teenage girl I've ever spoken to apart from my sisters. I wish she liked me, but I kind of understand why she doesn't. If I go by my screen experiences again, boys like me are usually ridiculed by their peers, and they certainly never get girlfriends. Joanna fixes her shiny dark eyes on me.

"I can't find anything," she says. "And what're you staring at, cross-eyes?"

"I'm not cross-eyed."

"You were checking me out, weren't you? I thought I made it clear on Facebook that I don't put up with that sort of thing."

"I wasn't checking you out," I say hastily. "I was just… thingy, you know, just . . ."

I can't think of what to say, so I shrug. Joanna rolls her eyes.

"And he says he's not retarded," she mutters before walking away. I want to follow her, but I can't move my legs. I try to call Joanna, to tell her I'm in trouble, but my mouth won't move either. As I watch Joanna go down the stairs, something crackles and hisses behind me. I want to see what it is but I can't turn my head. My entire body is rigid and cold. Then a whisper, *"Peregrine Zircon Gwithyas!"*

I know that voice. I've heard it before. I try to remember where and when I heard it, but I am interrupted by a snarling shriek, "Open the door, Gwithyas!"

This is a different voice, an unfamiliar one. Someone is giggling now. A child.

"Let us come and play," it says.

The whisperer intervenes. *"Be careful, Peregrine Zircon. Remember your duty."*

Duty? My head starts to hurt again and I hear cackling laughter and a grating voice shouting, "To hell with duties!"

And then there is the face. Well, not quite a face, it's just a cloud of frizzy dark hair and under that two gaping, almond-shaped empty eye sockets and a pair of beautiful lips that start to bleed as they speak, "Let us in, boy, and we will help you win the heart of that young lady. Literally, if you like."

Giggles again, and the pseudo-face dissolves into a blur. I've lost my glasses. How did that happen? The blur moves closer and speaks in a soft voice, "We can improve your eyesight, too. You'd look so much better without those goggles. We can do so much for you. All you have to do is let us in."

"Don't listen, Zircon. You have a responsibility."

Yes. Responsibility. I am the Guardian. I shouldn't let them in. What am I thinking? Dad's still alive, I'm not the Guardian yet! And I will never be. There is no such thing as a Guardian.

Delusions. Hallucinations. Insanity. The pressure inside my skull is so great now that I fear my head will split in two.

"Good boy, open up, just a little further."

"Hurry, Gwithyas!"

"She'll love you forever."

"Don't give in Zircon! Focus!"

Focus? On what? Oh yes. Mum talked about focusing on the gems. Only one gem left now: the little orange zircon, my namesake. It's still in my pocket. I try focusing on it, but someone is shouting at me, *"The doorway! The doorway! Don't let them through!"*

Through? Something is creaking, like the badly-oiled hinges of a door opening inside my head. Keep the doorway shut. Dad was so adamant, and yet I didn't oil the hinges. Oh, no. That was his office door. My mind is a mess. Never mind. It's all in the mind. My mind. Tiny little fingers, paper-white with blazing red claws, scratch over the door frame, feeling their way out. Or in. Out of the Void, and into my world.

"We are coming, Gwithyas."

No.

With all my might I push at the door. It bangs shut, and it feels as if someone hits me on the head with a cricket bat. I fall flat on my face on the wooden floor, and bright white flashes obscure my already lousy vision. My nose hurts. I try my arms. I'm relieved to find that I can move them, but they're hard to coordinate and it takes me great effort to push myself up to leaning on my elbows. My thoughts mist over and my head is spinning. I take a deep breath, and another. I don't want to pass out.

Slowly but surely I regain control over my body. I feel over the floor for my glasses and find them right next to me, fortunately not broken. I put them on, which hurts my wounded nose, and I sit up. Everything is normal. The room is an innocent structure of stone and wood, and it looks as if nothing ever happened in here. Perhaps nothing ever did. Perhaps I imagined it all. I heard non-existent voices, and saw an unreal face. Hallucinations. Symptoms of schizophrenia, what else could it be? I take another deep breath, and when I breathe out my glasses mist over with condensation.

Schizophrenic or not, I need to get out of here if I don't want to die from hypothermia. I struggle to my feet and stagger down the stairs. By the time I reach the garden I'm exhausted, and my nose is throbbing as badly as my head. I consider going straight to my bedroom but when I get outside I see that it's getting dark. How is that possible? I went up only an hour ago. Perhaps I did pass out after all. It must be nearly suppertime. I'm not at all hungry, but Mum might get worried if I don't turn up, and she can be a nuisance when she's worried. I shiver. The garden isn't that much warmer than the tower room. Winter will be early this year.

When I walk into the dining room Opal is there, laying the table. She looks up as I enter and she freezes, her hands with a small pile of plates hovering over the table. She presses her thin lips together so tightly that become nearly invisible, puts the plates down and walks over to me.

"You are hurt," she says. "What happened, Zircon?"

I open my mouth, but my lips tremble and I don't want to cry, so I say nothing. Opal takes my hand. "Come," she says, and it doesn't even occur to me to object.

She walks me over to the downstairs cloakroom, where she fishes a flannel out of the under-the-sink cabinet, holds it under the running tap, and then turns to me with the wet cloth.

"I'm going to clean you up," she says. "Your nose has been bleeding. It's all over your face."

I look in the mirror. Indeed, the bottom half of my face is covered in dried-up blood. I turn away. I never liked the sight of blood.

Opal gently cleans my face. Miraculously, the water she uses isn't freezing cold. Sometimes our boiler actually works.

"That's better," says Opal after a while. "How are you feeling?"

"I'm fine," I say—those words are rapidly becoming my

catch phrase—and I take another look in the mirror. I groan. My coke-bottle spectacles now rest on a swollen, shiny red blob of a nose. I look like a comical cartoon figure. I can't possibly show myself like this. Not to Joanna.

"Is it sore?" asks Opal.

"Kind of," I say, but I don't tell her that it isn't the pain that distresses me most.

"I don't think it's broken," says Opal. "It'll probably feel and look a lot better by tomorrow. Come, let's have supper."

"I'm not hungry."

"You haven't eaten anything at all today," says Opal.

She's right; I haven't. But I'm still not hungry. I feel absolutely miserable. My head is not clear. Those horrid voices are still echoing menacingly in my mind. I shudder.

Opal softly rubs my arm, looks into my eyes, and asks quietly, "What happened, Zircon?"

She looks kind of watery, probably because I'm seeing her through a mist of tears. I sniffle, and then, without intending to, I tell her everything.

"We were in the tower. There were voices. They told me to open the door. They ripped me. Ripped my mind. There was a face with no eyes. They were coming through, scratching inside my head, and I shut the door, and then I fell on my nose." As I say all this, I hear how utterly insane it sounds, but the only thing my sister asks is, "Wasn't Joanna with you?"

"No," I say. "She left. She got annoyed with me. Opal, I was hallucinating. And it's not the first time either. I'm losing my mind. I'm going mad."

Opal is still stroking my arm. Only a week ago I'd have been horrified, and so would she, at the mere idea of her showing me this much compassion. But now it seems right, and, worse, I need it.

"You're not mad, Zircon Gwithyas," she says. "Not at all. But if you don't eat, you *will* become ill. Come."

So I end up at the table. It is set for four only.

"Is Joanna not coming?" I ask. "Did she leave?"

"No," says Amethyst, who looks at me as concerned as Opal. "Joanna will be here, but Mum is staying upstairs. I took her and Dad's dinner up a few minutes ago."

"Oh," say, and I pull my glasses down to feel if my nose is a bit less swollen. It isn't. It actually feels bigger than before, and any moment now Joanna will be here, and she'll see me like this. Perhaps I'd do better to eat in my bedroom too, like Mum and Dad. I consider this, but the prospect of climbing another staircase sends shivers through my still flimsy legs, so I stay at the table. What does it matter anyway, Joanna already thinks I'm gross, she said so herself. My mangled appearance won't make her opinion of me any worse.

Then she enters the room, looks at me, and asks, "What have you done to yourself?"

I hesitate. I should of course tell her that I've been hallucinating in the tower and got so scared that I fell on my nose, but I have a better idea. Perhaps I can make this work for me by adding a hint of coolness to my otherwise pathetic personality.

"I was skateboarding," I lie. "I was trying this new trick, the double flick flack, and I fell. I reckon I'll get it right next time."

Opal coughs and Amethyst pats Opal on her back. I avoid looking at them. They know quite well that I can barely keep my balance on the broken step at our back door. Also, I'm not sure if flick flack is actually a skateboarding term. I take the gamble that Joanna doesn't know either. She snorts.

"Skateboarding," she scowls. "Skateboarding and computer games. You sure know your priorities, don't you? As long as prince Zircon has his fun, it doesn't matter if his parents are ill, his sisters do the housekeeping and his guest tries to prevent the end of the world. You're such a spoiled, immature brat."

So much for making a cool impression.

Amethyst serves the food. She's done the cooking today.

Jacket potatoes and baked beans. I normally love that, but now I struggle to get in more than two bites of potato and a spoonful of beans. Opal and Amethyst eat ant portions as usual. Only Joanna dives in with gusto.

"I was starving!" she says, and then, "I missed lunch. While you were out trying your new tricks, I telephoned my uncle to tell him about the situation here. He said it doesn't add up. He was surprised when I told him the Guardian was your father, because he had expected someone younger."

"Like Zircon," says Amethyst.

"Like any of you," says Joanna. "It doesn't have to be Zircon. You're triplets, aren't you?"

"Yes," says Opal. "But Zircon is the oldest. He's next in line to be the Guardian. Then me, and then Amethyst."

"It doesn't matter," says Joanna dismissively. "Your father's still alive, so he's now the Guardian and I am to be his shield."

She pops a large spoon full of beany potato in her mouth and while chewing she mumbles, "He also fsaid, my uncle I mean, he fsaid that according to the premonitions he's had . . ."

"Premonitions?" I interrupt her. "Is your uncle a psychic or what?"

Joanna swallows her food and eyes me broodingly over her plate. "He is, in fact. More a medium actually. The spirits speak to him."

I huff. Apparently insanity is not limited to my family.

"We speak to the spirits too," says Opal, casting a reproachful glance at me. "What did they tell your uncle?"

Joanna looks at her plate and says, "Nothing very nice. I'm sorry. They said that by the time I got here, hell would be about to break loose. Like, literally. The old Guardian would come to a gruesome end—I guess that's correct, that'd be your Nanny—and then the new Guardian would be suffering from ill health, which is the case with your father, and he'd be unable to keep the door shut. Of course if that happens the world would be flooded with Koeg. But that isn't happening though, is it? Look at us, sitting at the table eating potatoes and beans. That's hardly a life-threatening situation, now is it? So I'm not sure what to make of that."

"Nanny wasn't a Guardian," says Amethyst. "Only our father is, and he is still alive."

"Even worse then," says Joanna. "My uncle's prophecy doesn't make any sense at all in that case."

"Unless," Amethyst shuffles her feet under the table. She always does that when she is thinking. "The spirits aren't so good at estimating time-frames," she says, and Opal adds, "So they could have been a few days off."

"Or years!" Amethyst says hastily.

"So you mean that you think Dad will die soon?" I ask.

"I did say or years!" insists Amethyst.

"He won't die from a concussion," I say. "And anyway, I think this entire thing has gone too far now. I don't find it acceptable to discuss my parents' dying because of some utterly insane superstition."

"I don't think your parents will die soon, Zircon," says Joanna. "I wouldn't worry about that. Do you know why?"

The tone of her voice promises little good, so I don't answer. It isn't necessary anyway. Joanna doesn't need my encouragement to vent her opinions.

"I know that, because if your father died, you would be the Guardian, Zircon." She leans over the table so she is closer to me. "My uncle always told me that the Guardian would a bright, courageous person with amazing powers, someone who selflessly makes many personal sacrifices, and who suffers greatly to meet their responsibilities to protect others. Someone to look up to. Now I don't want to insult you . . ." She stops, shakes her head, and corrects herself, "Actually I don't care if I insult you. You are a spoiled, pampered whimpering baby and you only think about yourself. You wouldn't know responsibility if it was rubbed into your face. I can't believe you'd ever be the Guardian. I don't want to believe it, because if you were, this world is doomed."

Now that hurts more than my nose. I open my mouth to say something back, but as usual I can't think of anything. Besides, a lump in my throat prevents me from speaking. So I just shrug. For some reason, that really annoys Joanna. When she fixes her now blazing eyes on me she resembles my idea of Medusa.

"You make me absolutely sick," she says in a low voice. "I've never seen such a stupid, useless . . ."

"That's enough."

Opal and Amethyst are both standing up. Literally: they are getting onto their feet, but also figuratively: they are standing up for me. Which is good, because at the moment my ability to be assertive is seriously compromised.

"You are a guest here," Amethyst points out. "You have no right to insult our brother like this in his own home. Or anywhere. He deserves better, so much better. You don't know half of it, Joanna Egwueke."

And then I do something utterly stupid.

"Yeah, and you better like me a bit more," I say. "Especially if you believe in all that rubbish with doorways and Guardians and all that. There is an enchanted family tree, you know, and on that you are jotted down as my wife. So there."

I can almost hear my sisters cringe. Joanna stiffens up. Her almond eyes turn into tiny slits, and when she speaks her voice is hoarse.

"Never," she says. "I'd rather be devoured alive by those Koeg."

She pushes her chair back and storms out of the room. So much for romance. I snort. Ouch. Damned nose.

"Oh Zircon," sighs Opal.

I get up. "I'll go see how Dad is," I say to my sisters.

CHAPTER 8
Inheritance

I DIDN'T LIKE IT WHEN JOANNA TALKED ABOUT THE OLD GUARDIAN coming to a horrible end, especially not with Nanny already dead, but I'm not overly worried. Premonitions are nonsense after all. There's no such thing as foretelling the future. The blatant errors in Joanna's story are clear evidence of that. Even if I'd be wrong and the premonitions are right, my father wouldn't be at risk, because there is another Guardian who has already died. Uncle Ronald. It fits almost perfectly; Uncle Ronald is the Guardian who died, and my Dad the one who suffers from poor health. I don't quite understand why Joanna would be Dad's shield though. I thought my Mum was that already. Perhaps he needs two shields now that Nanny is dead. Yes, that makes sense. Sense?

I call myself to order. None of this is true, it can't be. It's nothing but superstition. This whole thing about Koeg from the Void is probably invented by one of my ancestors to ward off burglars. Or, more likely, mental health carers.

Of course I did see the face, and I heard the voices. That doesn't mean they're real, it only means that I am mentally ill. Or maybe not. Maybe I dreamt it. Maybe I just fell, hit my head and passed out in the tower room. That would explain this grating headache too. Yes. That must be it. All this idiocy is down to a combination of superstition and health problems. Now that's a sensible, satisfactory explanation. But I still want to see my parents.

I knock on their bedroom door. No answer. I knock again, and I say, "Mum? Can I come in?"

Nothing.

"I came to get your plates," I lie. "Amethyst told me you've eaten in here."

Still nothing. Perhaps they dozed off. I carefully push down the door handle and peek into the room. It's not dark in there, because my mother's reading light is on. She must've fallen asleep while reading. Her long grey-blonde hair is spread over her pillow like a halo. Dad's lying next to her, but since he boasts a crew cut there's no spreading of hair there. The dinner plates are on the bedside table, both of them, and they're full. My parents haven't eaten. Understandable. I had no appetite either.

I tiptoe into the room, my eyes focused on my parents. They must be exhausted, because they're not moving even the slightest bit. They must also be getting chilly since their double duvet is lying on the floor next to the bed in a messy heap. Dad is wearing nothing but a t-shirt and boxers, and Mum is dressed in a blouse and jeans. That's unusual. She always puts on pyjamas before she goes to bed. I wonder what made her forget to do that. Perhaps Dad is feeling better, and the reason they are both in bed is of a less worrying, more repulsive nature. Ew. I don't want to think such things about my parents, they're far too old. I stop walking and stand on the bedroom rug for over a minute, staring at my parents. They still don't move. I clear my throat, but there's no reaction. They must be in a very deep sleep. By the time they wake up their food will be cold and unpalatable. I think it's better to take the plates away. I look at the full plates, and then at my silent parents. Too silent. And they should've eaten, really, they're so thin. Skin over bone. Literally. The shapes of their skeletons stand out under their wrinkled skins. Dad's stubble stands up like a hedgehog's spines on his grey cheeks, and Mum's lipstick forms a small pink ring around her bared teeth. They are not sleeping, their hollow eye sockets are wide open.

I don't know how long I stand there looking at my mother and father. I'm hot, cold and numb, all at the same time.

Someone giggles behind me. I turn around and see a little girl. Tight pigtails with white ribbons, rosy cheeks and an old-fashioned embroidered frock. She can't be older than six or seven.

"You can do whatever you like and they won't tell you off!" she says, and she picks up an ornament, a china statuette of a sleeping dog. "You could even juggle with this," she says, and she throws the statuette in the air, crosses her arms and giggles when the china dog shatters on the floor. "Even if you break it they won't mind."

"My mother likes that sculpture," I say. "She says it reminds her of the pet dog she had when she was little."

"Liked," giggles the girl. "Said. Reminded. Past tense. She's dead. Dead. Dead. Dead." She smiles at me. "My mummy is dead too, and my daddy," she says, and her smile makes way for a pouting bottom lip. "I'm a little orphan, like you. I killed my mummy and daddy, and I helped to kill yours. Poor Peregrine Zircon Gwithyas. You don't need to be alone. I have friends, many friends, and they all want to play with you."

She moves a little closer. I back away. Why? She's only a little girl who's talking a lot of rubbish.

"I have something of yours," she says, and she opens her hand. In it lies the orange zircon. I touch my trouser pocket and sure enough, it's no longer there. I must've lost it when I was in the tower earlier. My focus, the link. Uncle Ronald told me it was important. I don't think I should let this girl know that.

"So what?" I bluff. "It's only a stone."

The girl folds her fingers over the gem and shakes her head. "No. Not just a stone, not just any old stone. No no no."

She shakes 'no' so hard that her head turns backwards, and

forwards again, 360 degrees, like in the film 'The Exorcist'. It makes me dizzy.

"Stop that!" I say.

The head stops instantly, but it's the wrong way around. The girl turns her back to me so she can see me, and she cocks her backwards head to one side.

"Don't you want to play, Gwithyas? It'll be fun. We know nice games. Let us come through."

She reaches out to me. Her hand is pink, smooth and chubby. Not at all like… I look over my shoulder at my emptied parents lying dry and stiff in their bed.

"They're gone, Gwithyas," says the girl. "They left you all alone. So you better let us in."

She's now in front of me, floating with her feet off the ground. Her blue eyes are glowing and her rosebud lips are stretched into an eerie snarl.

"Hurry, Gwithyas," she says, and I see stars. No, not stars. Flashes of bright white light surrounded by deep black halos.

"Let us in. My friends will come out to play. It will be fun."

I heard those words before. No, not heard. I read them. In a letter, with abominable spelling. Cecilia. My creepy ancestor. Hah. I won't be eaten by her friends.

"No," I say.

She growls and is no longer cute and pink. Her hand, now a bloody ribbon of muscles and tendons, slips into the sleeve of my jumper, and her claws pierce my skin and dig into my flesh. Cecilia drags me up until I'm dangling over my dead parents, with my blood dripping from my arm through my sleeve onto Mum's blouse. Mum's fawn-coloured blouse with flower print of which she said that it compliments her eyes. She wouldn't want stains on it.

"Let us in!" screeches the little girl, who now is neither little nor girl, and pain rams into my head, crushing my thoughts. I scream. At least I try to, but it's like that time in the cellar: I cannot hear my own voice. Someone is pulling my hair, bending my head back so I'm forced to face up at the ceiling. The plasterwork of the old ceiling rose has cracked open and there is now a black hole there, with blood and bits of ragged flesh falling out of it onto my parents' white plush carpet. A sickly grey hand slides out and reaches for my face.

"We're coming, Gwithyas!"

I try to turn my face away when the diseased claw touches my cheek, but I can't move.

Someone shouts, "Oh my God!" It's underneath me. Joanna. What the hell is she doing here?

"Stop them!" she cries. "Stop them, Zircon! They're entering our world!"

As if I didn't know. I wish she'd tell me how she reckons I should stop them, that'd be more useful. I feel the claw fold around my head and then I'm being shaken like a ragdoll.

"Let us through!"

"No, Zircon! Don't!" shouts Joanna, and she leaps up next to me and slashes her sword at the intruders. The screeching intensifies and the claw withdraws from my head, but I don't get the chance to feel relief. While this claw disappears, the one in my arm starts to scratch at what I assume to be my radius. I need to ignore it. I need to think. That's more easily decided than done. The pain in my arm is awfully distracting and my mind is a garbled mess. Focus. What was it? What should I do again? Nanny was the lock. My father is dead. I am the Guardian. The door is open. That's why my head hurts. The door is in my head, the hole in the ceiling is only an illusion. The Koeg are entering this world through me.

The pain is becoming too much. I'm going to faint. I wish Mum and Dad were here to help me, but they are nothing but bones covered with leather; lifeless mannequins of horror. Bog bodies. The Koeg killed my parents because I wasn't doing my job. They'll kill everyone. Me, my sisters, the nasty lady from the chemist, Ms. Chen the optometrist, the librarians, the bullying teenagers, the smelly guy from DVD rentals, the town gossips, my forum friends, even Joanna.

I can't let that happen. I need to stop them, and I can come up with only one way. Let's see how they enter our world if the door is stuck on their side. I jump, and then I fly through the hole in the ceiling. And then there is nothing.

CHAPTER 9
Void

The first thing I become aware of is yet more pain. My head hurts, and my nose, and now also my arm. The second thing I notice is a pungent odour. It's something I've smelled before, but I can't place it. All I know is that it's wrong. I shouldn't be smelling this. I try to open my eyes but fail. Probably wouldn't do me much good anyway, since I don't seem to be wearing my glasses. So I remain in the dark, in pain and in the stench. And worst of all: alone.

I wish Mum were here, but she can't be, and neither can Dad. Empty sockets in skins over bones on flowery sheets. That's all that's left of them. I'm an orphan. I'm alone.

"Not alone, brother."

Opal. I cannot see her, but I feel her presence, and Amethyst's too.

"We're here," says Amethyst, and she brushes through my hair to soothe my headache.

"We always will be," says Opal, and she blows softly over my arm to ease the pain.

"Perpetua Presencia. We are always with you, Peregrine Zircon. Brave Gwithyas."

I open my eyes. As anticipated, I see only a hazy blur. I'm

lying on my stomach on a hard wooden floor with my face in a gooey puddle. A smelly gooey puddle. I move my head, and some of the goo enters my nose. Eugh. I need to get out of this as soon as possible.

I push myself up, which isn't easy since my body parts seem to have forgotten how to work together and I cannot use my left arm at all. It takes me several attempts before I manage to sit up. No idea what to do next. I try looking around, but that's kind of pointless without my glasses. Glasses. Of course, the glasses. Find the glasses. That's always the first move. They must've fallen, so, by logical deduction, they must now be on the floor.

I stay where I am and move my hand over the floorboards. The floor is covered in a sticky substance that glues itself onto my fingers. It's gross and I don't even get any results. My glasses aren't here. I lean forward to feel a little further away. Still no glasses, but I do find something else. Fabric stretched over something that's solid, soft and warm. A human body part, a leg most likely. I pat it and am answered by a grunt. It sounds familiar.

"Joanna?"

Movement. And then a sizzling, resounding slap against my head. "Get off me you creep!"

Great. More pain. I rub my head.

"Sorry," I say. "I'm really sorry. I didn't mean to be offensive. I lost my glasses so I can't see."

"Where the hell are we?"

Joanna's on her feet before I can even consider an answer, and I hear her huff as she bends over, probably to get her sword.

"I d-don't know," I stammer. "My glasses are gone."

She presses something in my hand. "Here," she says. "A little bent, but still functional. And sorry about the slap. It was a gut reaction."

I put my spectacles on and finally get to see my surroundings. We're definitely not in my parents' bedroom. This place is much bigger. And it's irregularly and illogically shaped, as if it wasn't built, but instead accidentally fell together.

"Well?" asks Joanna, "Where are we?"

"I don't know."

I let go of my glasses. They are sticky, and so are my fingers. I look at them. They're red. Blood. Of course, my arm bled when that girl-monster ripped it. But surely not this much? One droplet falls from my finger and I follow its journey down until it lands in more dark red liquid. The entire floor is covered in blood. And not only the floor. It's also dripping from the walls. So that's the unsettling odour: blood, but in such vast amounts that I couldn't place the smell.

"This is gross!" I whimper.

"Think so?" asks Joanna. "Then I suggest you get up quickly, 'cause it's soaking your trousers."

I jump up—a bad move, because immediately I see a fountain of stars. I don't want to fall back in the pool of blood so I reach out to lean against the wall. My hand splashes into the oozing blood, which makes me feel even more ill.

Joanna doesn't react to my struggle to stay upright and conscious, and when I am clear-headed again I see that she's staring at the ceiling, her head bent back so that her fuzzy brown hair falls on the waistband of her jeans.

I look up to see what has her so entranced. From the ceiling dangles a collection of irregularly shaped objects, all of them deep red and dripping with blood. It takes me a few seconds to work out what they are. Flesh. Human body parts. Then I spot the eyes. There are four of them, dangling from thin bloody nerves, one pale grey set and one hazel brown. Eyes that have looked at me so many times, with love, concern, delight, and sometimes irritation, but now they no longer see me and they never will again. I keep looking at them, unable to avert my gaze, barely able to breathe.

"I know where we are," says Joanna. "This is the Void, where the Koeg are from. You went through the doorway, Zircon. What did you do that for?"

Mum. Dad. I want to tell her, tell Joanna, but the words get stuck in my throat. Joanna puts her hand on my head and pushes it down until I'm facing her. She frowns, and she says, "Take a deep breath, Zircon. Calm down."

Her voice is sweet and soothing, and I do as she says. She keeps her hand on my head until I stop shaking.

"Better?" she asks. I nod.

"Good," she says. "I'll ask you again: Why did you do it? Why jump through that door?"

I open my mouth, but I still can't get the words out. It's as if my tongue has turned to wood. So I shrug. Joanna's frown becomes deeper.

"Surely you must've had a reason. You're supposed to become a Guardian, remember? Your task would be to keep the Koeg out of our world, not to drag us into theirs!"

"I-I didn't!" I stammer, but then I remember that I did exactly that, and quite deliberately too. But it was meant to be only me.

"I didn't mean for you to go through as well," I say. "I'm sorry."

"That's a fat lot of help," says Joanna, but she doesn't sound angry. Her hand is now on my cheek. It's pleasantly warm. Not particularly soft. Joanna's hands have many hard-skinned patches, as you'd expect from a warrior. Her touch makes me feel, well, not quite safe, not here, but at least a little less hopeless. We stand there, motionless, until Joanna says, "We need to get out of here." She moves her hand off my face, twists on her heels and then points. "There."

It's a door. An extraordinarily ordinary wooden door. Joanna takes a few steps towards it and then stops.

"Aren't you going to open it?" I ask.

"We don't know what's behind there," she says.

I look at the blood-covered walls.

"That's true," I say. "But we do know what is on this side, and that isn't that great, is it?" I reach past her and push the handle down. The door swings open.

Now this is insane. Apparently Joanna thinks so too, and she expresses her feelings by uttering a word that would be beeped out in TV family shows.

"I didn't expect that," she says.

"Me neither," I reply.

We stand there, on the bloody planks, and take in the sight of lush green fields, soft blue sky, and bright sunshine. Quaint. Reassuring. Exactly the landscape where you'd expect a rosy-cheeked little girl with white-bowed braids to be running and skipping and laughing. There she is too, complete with white bows. Her blonde braids bounce while she runs and skips, but she isn't laughing. She stops a few feet away from the door.

"You didn't let us in," she says accusingly. "Naughty. Never mind. We can play here instead. Come, Gwithyas. I know a fun game."

"I don't think you do," I say. "I don't think you and I like the same games."

"You will like this one!" she insists. "Really. Just come."

My head starts to feel tense. The girl beckons me. "Come, Gwithyas."

I don't think I should. She's hardly trustworthy. But what other options are there? Staying here is pointless.

"Okay," I say, and I put my left foot on the grass.

Joanna breathes in sharply. "Zircon!" she hisses. "Don't!"

"Both feet!" insists the little girl.

"Use your sword if you need to," I tell Joanna, and I put my right foot on the grass as well.

There is no grass. In fact, there is nothing at all, so I fall, and then the voices are back, and they are screeching and howling and roaring, obviously going for a shock effect, but they fail. I'm not scared. Correction: I *am* scared, but not overwhelmed and in a complete panic. This time I expected them. Also, they don't sound as vicious as before. The howls in particular have a snivelling quality to them.

"Shut up!" I shout. "You won't scare me. You can't do anything. You killed my father, so now I am the Guardian, and I am here, in your world. I ruined your doorway!"

One more screech, and then it's silent and I'm floating. Or falling. It's cold, and very dark, and all I can see is the Koeg who approaches me. Or is it more than one? It's so big that it could easily be several individuals merged into one grotesque abomination. It has three heads, one of which comes so close to me that when it snorts, its acidic fumes tingle on my cheek. The head has no eyes, and where you'd expect a snout there is only a gaping, bloody hole.

"A mere setback," thunders a voice too low to hear. I know only what it's saying because the meaning vibrates through my brain, thumping against the inside of my skull. A rumble of laughter shakes my inner organs while the un-voice relentlessly carves its words into my shaky consciousness. "We merely have to wait a little longer. It will be worth it, for your anguish will be so much greater, Gwithyas."

The skull-thumping becomes harder and faster and shakes my brain into a mushy mass incapable of producing coherent thoughts, which the Koeg takes as an invitation to fill my head with its own reflections.

"We want you to suffer, Gwithyas," it trembles in my brain. "You will weaken, bit by bit you will lose your strength, your health, your coherency, and then we will rip your mind to shreds, and we shall open the door while you perish. It will be so much fun."

The head comes closer and the bloody edges of its mouth touch my face in a sickening distortion of a kiss. The blade of a sword flashes past me and the Koeg is torn off my cheek. I brace myself for an eternal tumble, but Joanna grabs me by my right arm and holds on to me while her sword sparks and slashes, and then there's a thud, and we are on solid ground.

I sink through my knees and end up sort of dangling on Joanna's arm. She's strong for a girl, and probably also for a boy, especially if that boy is a flimsy weakling like me, so she doesn't drop me. She slowly goes down until we're both sitting. She pulls me close to her chest, which is quite a pleasant experience, and then she pats my cheek. "Zircon?"

That's my name all right. I can see Joanna's face, twice even.

"Zircon!" she says again in a sharper tone while patting me a tad more vigorously than I would've liked. "Get a grip. Talk to me!"

Talk? There was a lot of talk. That Koeg was quite chatty for a creature with no proper mouth. It threatened me. Was that bluff or can they really do that? Rip my mind to shreds, and then go to the real world when I'm too weak to resist? I can't let that happen. A low groan escapes from my throat. I sound like a creaking door. Or perhaps it's not me at all. It dawns on me that I'm back in the blood room, and the door is slowly blowing open.

"Zircon?" Joanna sounds more uncertain now. I take a deep breath and my thoughts line up. No Koeg, all gone. My headache is fading. I clear my throat.

"I'm okay," I say.

That isn't entirely true, but Joanna seems satisfied.

"Can you stand up?" she asks.

"Yeah," I say, and I start to scramble up. Joanna holds me under my arms and helps me to my feet as if I'm some little old man.

"I'm fine," I say. "Really. Honestly. You can let go now."

Joanna raises her eyebrows, but she does let go of me and says, "Just let me know if you're not good, okay?"

I nod. Standing takes more effort than I had anticipated, and I don't feel up to talking. I notice that the door is wide open, but this time there is no outside. The door now opens into a corridor. A very normal corridor, not unlike the one that leads to the drawing room in my house. Only this one is longer. So long in fact that I can't see the end. Joanna peeks over my shoulder.

"Great," she says. "It's a never-ending hallway. Probably leads to more blood."

I touch the corridor's wall. It is cold, made of stone, and it's dry. No blood there. When I look up the ceiling is only a ceiling, with nothing dangling from it, not even cobwebs. The illusion of normality is shattered when I inspect the floor. One would expect it to be stone, or tiles, or even wood. It's none of these things. Initially I think it's just mud, but it is far too smooth, shiny even, and with a hint of nausea I realise that this floor pulsates rhythmically, as if it were a breathing organism. I shut my eyes, open them again, and the floor is still throbbing.

"It's a Koeg," I whisper.

"Where?" asks Joanna, and she twists on her heels, waving her sword about.

"There." I point at the floor. Joanna looks, swallows, and pokes at it with the tip of her sword. The tip sinks in, and is then forcefully pushed back, leaving behind a bleeding gash. Joanna gags. The Koeg floor—or is it a floor Koeg?—continues to pulsate quietly while the gash closes.

"So what do we do now?" I ask Joanna.

"What're you asking me for?"

That's a good question, actually.

"Because there's no one else?" I try.

"There's you," replies Joanna. "You're supposed to become a Guardian. And you're the one who got us here in the first place, so the least you could do is get us out, too."

She has a point, but it makes no difference. I still don't know what to do. I shuffle my feet, which causes some not-quite-dry blood to seep through the crumbling soles of my shoes so my socks become damp and sticky.

"Who was that girl?" asks Joanna. "The cute little one?"

"I wouldn't call her cute," I remark.

"She seemed cute at first," says Joanna. "And you seemed to know her."

"I've met her before. Only once. I think her name is Cecilia. She is . . . a relative of mine."

"A relative?"

"Yes."

"Right," says Joanna.

We both look into the corridor again.

"I guess we'll have to get in there," I say.

"You reckon?"

I glare at the pulsating Koeg. It looks less than appealing.

"Well," I say, "the other option is to stay here, in the blood room, and wait for the Koeg to come back."

Joanna presses her lips together. "Point taken," she says, and she steps into the corridor and starts to walk.

It looks easy when she does it, but when I try it, it's anything but. Every time I place a foot on the floor it sinks down about ankle deep, and then the Koeg bulges out and pushes the foot back up, as if it dislikes being stepped upon. It probably does. So I have to be quick, put one foot down before the first one is pushed up, or I'd fall. I don't know what would happen if I fell. I think it's quite likely that this floor would devour me whole. So I need to walk fast, there's no time to rest. It's a hard chore and it doesn't take long before my lack of physical fitness starts to take its toll. I huff and wheeze and my leg muscles become dense, aching clumps.

Joanna speeds along, moving further away from me with every bounce. I don't like her being so far away, but I dare not ask her to slow down. I mean; she was dragged into this pit of despair by me, so I'm hardly her favourite person. She's probably glad to have a break from me. So I don't call her and I just keep bouncing forward until my legs are so tired that they seem detached from the rest of my body. They're still working, but I can't feel them anymore. My mind too is detaching itself. It's as if I have always been here, bouncing in this endless corridor, and I'll be here forever.

No.

I am the Guardian, I need to find the find the way back, through the doorway. Hah. What am I thinking? Koeg. Guardian. Doorway. Only a few hours ago I would've disregarded all that.

I would've said it's all superstition. Perhaps it is. Perhaps I'm hallucinating. Perhaps I've really lost it now. Part of me hopes that is the case, because I don't particularly want my current situation to be real. I look around for a sign, any sign, that this morbid living tunnel isn't real, and that I'm actually still in the normal world, probably locked away in some asylum between four white walls, with stern nurses tending to me and jabbing needles full of sedatives into my twitching limbs.

That's when the arch appears. I'm sure it wasn't there when I looked the first time, but it is now: an opening set low in the wall on my left hand side, barely visible. Ahead of us is only the corridor, stretching into eternity for all I know.

"Maybe we should try this door," I pant, but Joanna doesn't reply, she's spotted the opening well before I did and is now busy judging its height and its distance from her, while bouncing from one foot to the other. She's made the decision already. She doesn't need me. Which is fine. I just wish I didn't need her either. Joanna arches her back and leaps through.

"Ouch!" she shouts, and then there is a frightening nothing, so I bounce closer and call through the opening, "Are you okay?"

"Yes," replies Joanna. "Floor's a bit hard, though. Make sure to put your arms out to break your fall when you jump in."

I stretch out my good arm, bend and push off with my feet. My jump is significantly less elegant than Joanna's. My bottom hits the high point of the arch and I plummet down with my feet still sticking out. I try to break my fall with my hand, but one arm isn't enough to hold my weight and my chin bangs onto smooth, hard tiles. Miraculously, my glasses don't come off. I wriggle over the tiles, desperate to get my legs in before that pulsating floor outside munches them up.

"Holy cow, Zircon," murmurs Joanna as she drags me in further. "It's not *that* hard!"

I sit up, huffing and puffing, and take in my new surroundings. A small room, square, with plain white walls and no windows. Exactly what you would expect of a patient's room in a psychiatric institution. My heart sinks. I wanted a sign. It couldn't be much clearer than this. I am nuts.

"Funny, isn't it?" asks Joanna. "It's just a normal room."

Then she's silent, waiting for me to give my opinion. I don't. It has now been proven that I'm insane, which means that Joanna is merely a figment of my demented imagination, so there's no need to talk to her. The figment rolls her eyes at me and brushes her hand over a wall.

"It's a wall," she says, and I cringe. Am I so boring that I can't even make my imaginary companions say something witty? Joanna continues feeling the white walls, feeling for, well, I don't know. Irregularities, I suppose. A secret door. A possible way out. Just like she did in the tower room.

I stay where I am and ignore her. I'm actually a bit angry at her for being not real. I know that isn't technically her fault, but it's still very misleading. And also, I genuinely have a crush on her, and if she's only an illusion—my illusion—she could have the decency to be a bit more forthcoming.

As she turns to the next wall, Joanna's hair bounces over the soft curves of her neck and shoulders. Real or not, she's damn pretty. I force myself onto my feet and shuffle over to her. It's not easy because my legs are horribly stiff. But I'm highly motivated. Since I am now certain that I'm a delusional schizophrenic, I know that my chances of ever kissing a real girl are negligible, so an imaginary kiss will have to do. The white room is tiny, so I'm next to Joanna in three or four shuffles.

"Joanna," I say.

"What?"

I put my hand on her cheek and bring my face closer to hers.

She frowns. "What are you doing?"

I ignore this auditory hallucination and pout my lips towards hers. Joanna recoils. I grab her by the sleeve and try to pull her towards me. She says something very rude, and then I can't breathe because Joanna has stomped me in the chest with her fist.

While I'm coughing and gasping she is screaming at me like

a harpy with a temper tantrum. This stinks big time. I can't even kiss a girl who only exists in my own mind. What does that say about my charm? I ignore Joanna's anger, which after all is only a reflection of my own, and I slide down against one of the walls. I want to pull my knees up against my chest but I can't. My legs are too stiff and achy. It's hard to find a comfortable position, and to make matters worse, the hallucinated Joanna just goes on and on, shouting at me in a high-pitched tone that irritates my ears.

"Oh shut up," I say.

Her eyes widen and spark with rage, and she hisses, "You really think you are something special, don't you?"

"I really think you should show me some more respect," I snap back, "or I will imagine you out of existence."

She blinks. "What are you talking about?"

"The correct question would be: why am I talking about it to you. You're not even real. None of this is. I'm mad. Insane, delusional. You're not real. I'm hallucinating."

Joanna looks at me with her lips so tightly pressed together that they change colour. Very unsettling.

"What?" I ask weakly. "You can go now. I figured you out. Leave me alone. "

She stands there, looks at me a while longer, and then says, "If you keep up that attitude, I will indeed leave you here and find a way out on my own. Just think that over while I explore this room."

She returns to feeling the walls. I doubt she'll find anything. It's not as if there's anything here that isn't plainly visible. Not that I care. I'm tired. I want to sleep. And why not? There's no need to be afraid. A psychiatric hospital is a lot safer than an alien world full of cruel Koeg.

I shut my eyes. Terrible idea. There is an instant tension in my head, and a thin grey tentacle slithers behind my eyes, scratching at my sockets. No fun at all. I try to open my eyes, but another tentacle holds them shut while the first one grows and increases in size until it's all over the inside of my face, and it's getting hot, and then there are piercing sniggers.

"Gwithyas . . ."

They touch my forehead. No, that's not them, this is a hand, a real hand. Suddenly the tentacles are gone, and I can open my eyes. Joanna is kneeling right in front of me, studying me with a probing look on her face, and she has her hand on my forehead.

"You're sick," she states.

"Yeah," I reply, "I'm insane. I already told you."

"I don't mean that." Her fingers tickle my forehead. "I think you have a fever," she says, and then she suddenly leaps to her feet and puts her finger on her lips.

"What?" I ask, startled.

"I hear something!" hisses Joanna, and she moves over to the door, sword ready for attack. She gestures me to be quiet, and then I hear it too. Voices. Not the eerie whispers and growls of the Koeg, or Cecilia's giggles, but men's voices, talking loudly. They come from the corridor just outside the arch.

"I'll go first," says one, and two hands come flying through the opening, followed by a flurry of blond hair. The man lands elegantly on the stone floor. He's young, a boy almost, not much older than I am. He gets on his knees, raises his head and sees me.

"What . . ." he starts, but Joanna presses the edge of her sword against his neck and he freezes.

"Hello," says Joanna. "Are you Koeg?"

The young man swallows. "No," he replies. "Are you?"

"No," says Joanna.

"I find that hard to believe," says the man.

"I'm not sure about you either," says Joanna, and she stays there, her sword at the man's neck while he kneels on the floor in what seems like a fairly uncomfortable position.

I feel sorry for him. I'm pretty sure he isn't Koeg. If he were he would've probably have shifted away from the sword by now, or changed into something horrible, and my head would be hurting.

"I don't think he's Koeg," I say to Joanna. "He doesn't feel like Koeg."

"Oh, now, that's really helpful, Zircon," says Joanna. "What do Koeg feel like then? Like failing to reach your highscore?"

"N-no," I say. "It's just that he's not giving me a headache."

Joanna squints at me, and that small moment of inattention is enough for the blond man. He rolls over the floor, away from the sword, and leaps up, all in one smooth motion. Then he is on his feet, facing Joanna, about to go for her sword, but she reacts even faster than he did and presses the tip of her sword on his throat.

"Don't move."

He wisely follows her advice and stands very still. "I'm not Koeg," he says again, "Believe your friend."

"He tends to be easily confused," growls Joanna.

I'm pleased that she didn't deny that I'm her friend.

"Well, he's right this time," says the man, and he swallows. That sword must be irritating his throat.

"You know I'm not lying," he says. "You can sense it, can't you? I'm as human as you are."

He smiles, and it strikes me that he's disturbingly handsome. Tall, muscular, with steel-grey eyes and strong, regular features. Joanna must've noticed it as well, because while she looks at him the expression on her face changes from angry to slightly dim.

"I've never seen a woman like you," says the man. "Such skin; like polished oak. And your hair . . ." He touches Joanna's hair and she continues to gaze at him.

"You must be Welsh," decides the man. "A dark, curvy beauty from the rugged mountains."

Joanna snorts and pushes her sword harder against his neck. "Don't think you can charm your way in here."

"I wouldn't stand a chance," he replies, still smiling in spite of the sharp blade that now appears to be pressing against his carotid artery. "You are clearly of noble descent. You are so high above me that all I can do is crumple in humility."

It's clearly fake, not to mention repulsive, but Joanna completely falls for his sentimental ramblings. She even smiles when the blond man cautiously pushes her sword away and says, "I beg you. Believe me. I am a man, a real man. Trapped in the Void like yourself."

Joanna slowly pulls her sword away. The man sticks out his hand.

"I'm Nathaniel," he says. "It's a joy to see another human for a chance. Especially such a beautiful one."

Joanna takes his hand, says her name and giggles. Nathaniel points at the arch to the corridor.

"My friend is still outside," he says. "Hopping on that giant floor Koeg. He must've heard us speak and waited to hear what would happen. Can I call him in without you slashing off his head?"

Joanna nods. When Nathaniel kneels down to call through the opening she looks at him with wide, moist eyes and a faint smile around her flustered lips. The way I had imagined she'd look at me.

Nathaniel stands up. He smiles a dazzlingly white set of teeth at Joanna and then takes her hand to move her out of the way. His friend jumps in and lands even more elegantly than Nathaniel had done, probably because he is a lot shorter. He is also a lot older, at least in his late twenties, and he has a bushy black beard and even bushier eyebrows. He is holding a brown bag that he drops while he gets up. It makes a sloppy sound when it hits the floor.

The man ignores the bag as he peers at Joanna. His eyes follow the line of her arm to her hand, which is still clutched by Nathaniel. Nathaniel quickly lets go. Is it my imagination or does his face turn a bit red? The bearded man frowns, not a pleasant sight with hedgehog eyebrows like his, and focuses his piercing black eyes on Joanna's face.

"Who's she?"

His voice is deep and a little threatening. Joanna takes a step back. Her knuckles turn yellow when she tightens her grip around the hilt of her sword.

"Her name is Joanna," says Nathaniel. "Another poor lost soul. You could be a little more welcoming, Jago."

Jago? The name rings a bell. As does Nathaniel, actually. I've seen or heard those names before. While I'm trying to jog my memory Jago de-frowns his face.

"Is she human?" he asks. "She looks odd."

"She is Welsh," says Nathaniel, and Jago nods understandingly while offering Joanna his hand. "Welcome," he says. "For what it's worth." Then he looks at me. "And who's that?"

I'm still sitting on the floor, so I quickly scramble up, but before I get round to opening my mouth, Joanna introduces me. "He's Zircon," she says. "He got us into this life-forsaken place."

Great. I didn't even get a chance to try and make a positive impression. Blemished from the very beginning. Never mind. I probably deserve it.

Nathaniel observes me as if I am an unusual specimen of an exotic species. I decide it's best if I stay near my wall.

"Sorry," I mutter, "I'm not so sociable."

Now they're all staring at me. I wish I knew what they are thinking. Or not. It probably isn't particularly flattering. I avoid their eyes. Nathaniel is the first to break the silence.

"Well, then," he says. "Have you yet discovered our secret entrance?"

"What secret entrance?" asks Joanna bewildered.

Nathaniel prods at the wall behind him, the only bit that Joanna had not yet examined, and it moves. It's not a wall, but a thick, white curtain, and behind it is another room.

"Our home," says Nathaniel. "Come in, lovely lady. You must be thirsty by now. And . . ." He wrinkles his perfectly shaped nose. "You could do with a wash."

All three of them disappear behind the curtain. I hesitate, not sure if I'm invited as well. I stand against the wall and I wait. I hear them talk, but can't make out what they're saying. I wait a little longer, but no one comes back. Apparently I'm not welcome.

I slide down and sit on the floor. I still cannot pull my knees up. I don't know what hurts more: my legs, my arm or the fact that I'm being discarded like a piece of rubbish. My cheeks are getting wet. I'm crying. It doesn't matter, I'm alone now, no one will see. I let my tears flow freely, and wipe my snotty nose on my sleeve.

CHAPTER 10
Socialising

"WELL HELLO THERE!"

An ape is looking down at me. A skinny, smelly primate with a familiar face. He is holding a DVD in each of his six hands.

"Want to rent a film?" he asks.

I recognise him. It's the guy who runs the DVD shop, or something that resembles him anyway. The ape doesn't wait for a reply but tosses a DVD at me.

"Alone in the World," he says. The film that lands in my lap is an animated version of Hector Malot's novel. The main character, the orphan Remi to whom the title refers, looks suspiciously like me.

"No," says the ape. "That story has a happy ending. That isn't realistic. This is more like it."

He flings another film at me. Its cover boasts an image of a little girl with a bloodied axe in her hands, and it's titled 'The truth about Lizzie Borden. A documentary.'

"She killed her parents," explains the ape. "Just like you."

"I didn't..." I start, but the ape doesn't let me speak.

"Time to drop the cover and show the truth," he snarls, and he sheds his skin, which falls on the floor in a rubbery heap.

"Well?" says the ape, his bare neck muscles pulsating. "Your turn."

"No!" I say. "I didn't kill them. It was you. It were the Koeg. I know who you are, you know."

"I know you know!" mocks the ape. "Did you hear that?"

I am about to reply that of course I heard it, I said it myself, but then I realise he wasn't talking to me, but to the platinum-blonde growth that is developing on his abdomen.

"He knows you know!" repeats a woman's voice.

The growth falls off the ape to become a woman's head that sticks its tongue out at me. The tongue morphs into a tiny body wearing a white uniform and a badge that says it's a fully-trained apothecary assistant. The body wriggles its long pink fingernails at me.

"Gwagh gwogh," says the blonde head. Apparently even in the Void you can't speak clearly with your mouth full.

The head swallows its tongue-body and says, "You blame the Koeg, but the Koeg only exist in your deranged mind, Gwithyas. So who is the murderer now?"

"You are, Gwithyas," confirms the ape. "You are evil. And nuts. You might just as well admit it. What would your precious Joanna say if she knew, eh?"

"Go away," I say.

"You don't have to be so miserable, you know," says the apothecary head. "You could work with us."

The ape leans over to me so his blood drips on my trousers. "You could be free," he whispers. "Or do you like it here, Gwithyas? Do you want to remain here, in Graham's nightmare, sick, lonely and rejected?"

I press my hands on my ears, but the voices continue inside my head, *"Let us through!"*

Do they really think I'll give in so easily? Hell no. I remember the skulls in the old kitchen. And my parents. So many innocent deaths, and those were the result of only short visits of the

Koeg. I don't want to find out what would happen if I gave those aberrations complete freedom.

"No," I say.

The ape lashes at my face. I duck to evade his sharp claws. The ape steps backwards, readying himself for another whack but then somebody grabs my hands and pulls me up.

"Run, Zircon!"

"Through the curtain! Run!"

My sisters. They promised they wouldn't leave me. I do as they say: I run. The white curtain flails open as I dash into the room behind it. I can't see where I'm going. I run, stumble, fall, and then someone catches me.

"Easy, boy!"

"Run!" I shout. "The ape! The head!"

"Not here," says a deep voice. "They're not here, easy, easy."

Two strong arms hold me up, which is a good thing because my legs are as unreliable as mouldy fence posts in a windstorm. I look up and see a mass of dark hair around two deep-set eyes. Jago. The bearded man.

"You're safe," he says. "Calm down."

He pulls me against his chest and holds me until I stop shaking and whimpering. When I come to my senses again I step back, wipe my nose and mumble, "Sorry."

"You have nothing to be sorry for," says Jago. "It's us who are to blame. We should never have left you alone." He puts an arm over my shoulders. "Come. Let's sit you down and get you a drink."

"Drink," I echo, and I meekly allow myself to be guided by Jago.

We walk through the room. The Void is not exactly void here, but crammed full with piles of boxes, chests and unidentifiable objects. We manoeuvre between them until we get to a brick fireplace. The clutter that is present in every corner of this room has been arranged to form improvised seats in front of the dancing fire. Joanna and Nathaniel are already here, sharing a trunk, laughing and chatting. They look up when we enter. Joanna opens her mouth, but shuts it without saying anything and then continues to laugh with Nathaniel.

Jago leads me to the fire. "Sit down, lad."

I select the seat that's furthest from Joanna and Nathaniel. When I sit down on it, Nathaniel casts a quick curious glance at me before turning his attention back to Joanna. I fix my eyes on my feet and don't look up until Jago hands me a small bowl filled with a hot, light brown liquid. Tea? Here, in the nothingness?

"Drink," orders Jago.

He sits down next to me. I sniff the drink. It smells of cinnamon, smoke and possibly alcohol. Not tea then. I'm not sure if I should drink it. I can't believe that a product from the Void could be beneficial to my health. Then I spot a similar bowl in Joanna's hands, and it's half empty. Well, she certainly seems perky enough. I take a sip. The stuff is a bit bland, but not bad.

While I drink, Jago gazes dolefully into the fire and Joanna and Nathaniel talk and giggle without interruption. I can't understand how they can be so relaxed and cheerful. Especially Joanna. Has she already forgotten that we're stranded in the Void with no way back? That didn't take much then, only pair of steel grey eyes and some supple muscles. Women. Always complaining about the superficiality of men and saying how it's the inside of a woman that matters, not the outside. Then when they have a choice, they themselves will keenly pick the muscular stud over the scrawny nerd. I suppress the nasty little voice—Koeg or my own thoughts?—that suggests that perhaps Nathaniel is also superior to me on the inside, and I drink my alcoholic smoked cinnamon tea.

After the drinks Joanna has a wash. She comes back dressed in an oversized but blood-free brown top and trousers. I can't understand this. There shouldn't be anything here, but they have a fire, bowls, clothes, and drinks. Joanna walks over to me and tilts her head.

"You should have a wash too," she says. "You're positively filthy."

I can't deny that. I can smell myself, and it isn't a joyous affair. But like with the drinks, I have my doubts. I'm not sure if I should wash myself with water that shouldn't exist and then get dressed in imaginary clothes. It's downright wrong. I can't believe that Joanna accepts it all as if it's normal.

"You'll feel better when you're clean," she insists. Then she sits down next to me and clears her throat. "I, ehm, I wanted to say sorry. I know I've been grumpy with you, but that was only because . . ." She shrugs, sighs and plucks at her fingernails. "Because I don't understand," she finally says. "And you're not helping me understand either. You're just bumbling about as if you're not even trying to find a solution. And why did you go through the doorway, Zircon? You never explained that. I do think I have a right to know, don't I? After all, it kind of messed up my entire life, didn't it? And yours."

She keeps looking at me, her eyes pleading, and I think she even briefly touches my fingers. I could tell her now. She doesn't seem angry, just kind of drained. It's easy. I open my mouth and tell her that my father died, and my mother, and that I had to stop the Koeg, and I didn't know what else to do, and that I'm injured, and that I didn't know that Joanna would be dragged through the doorway too, and I didn't want that to happen.

That is what I want to say, but before I get the words out I recall what the ape and the head said: that it is my fault, that I am the one who killed my parents, and also the one who's keeping Joanna trapped in this deranged dump, and that she will hate me and resent me once she knows that, and all I end up saying is, "I'm sorry."

Joanna doesn't budge. I know she is waiting for me to say more, but there is nothing else I can say without making matters worse. After a while Joanna sighs and stands up.

"Fine," she says. "If that's the way you want it. At least have a wash. You stink."

She walks around the fire with long steps, back to Nathaniel.

"Do you want to have a wash?" asks Jago, who is sitting on my other side.

I might as well. I nod, and Jago gets up.

"I'll show you where."

I fiddle my legs about but they're so stiff now that it's hard to move them. Jago sticks his big hands under my arms and puts me on my feet.

"Thanks," I mutter, slightly embarrassed. "I'm a bit stiff."

Jago stays close to me while we walk to the far wall. There's a low door, made of shiny wood. I touch it. It's smooth and cold. Not wood then. It reminds me of the material on which the family tree was drawn.

"What is this stuff?" I ask.

"Door," says Jago.

He must think I'm daft.

"Yes," I reply. "I meant: what is it made of?"

Jago's beard twitches. That may indicate that he's smiling.

"It's made of pure door. Once you smell better I'll explain."

The door opens onto wide steps that lead to a dark, windowless space, not so much a room as a cave. Its rough dark walls blend seamlessly into the equally rough dark ceiling.

"The kitchen," says Jago.

Kitchen? The Void must've gotten to him, because I don't see the tiniest trace of cooking equipment. In fact, the room is empty except for a massive fireplace in the far wall, a well, and a pile of fabrics. There's also a rope sticking out of the well. Jago grabs it and pulls up a bucket full of water, which he puts down in front of me. Then he points to the pile of fabrics.

"Towel and clothes."

Towels. I can't hold back a smirk. In this cursed, surreal realm of emptiness there are towels.

"Thank you," I say.

Jago folds his thick black eyebrows into a serious frown. "Will you be all right?"

I assure him I will be.

"I'll be right outside if you need help," he replies, and he leaves me behind in his grim kitchen.

In hindsight I could've done with some help. It takes me ages to take off my blood-soaked clothes. But I don't call Jago. I don't want them all to think that I'm a useless little squib, if that's not what they're thinking already. But I also don't want anyone to see my wounds because that might lead them to ask questions that I'd rather not answer.

I peel my sleeve from my injured arm, bit by bit. The fabric sticks to the crusts that have formed over the gashes and pulls them off, which is both gross and painful. I grit my teeth and keep peeling until finally my jumper slides heavily on the floor and I can see my arm. Three long cuts run over its inner side, from my wrist to just under my elbow, and where the crusts came off the flesh is exposed. There's a white thing there too—maybe a bit of bone? Gross. I look away and let my gaze wander over the floor.

The floor isn't plain stone like the rest of the room. In fact it's very neatly tiled. Smooth, black tiles. I get a sense of déjà vu. I've been here before. I know I have, but before I can get a grip on the memory it slips back into the deepest, foggiest crevices of my brain. Whatever. It doesn't matter, and it probably wasn't an actual memory anyway. This room is likely only familiar because I'm hallucinating it with my own mind.

I tidy myself as well as I can with one hand while avoiding touching my wounds and when I'm more or less clean and dry I get on with the daunting task of putting on the brown clothing. The clothes are too big. They must be Nathaniel's. All the better. It means that they slide on easily, and who knows, some of Nathaniel's charm may rub off on me and Joanna might like me better. The clothes are of a soft, silky material that falls warm and smooth against my skin. Once I'm dressed I feel a little more human, but also pretty exhausted. I leave the kitchen-cave and find Jago waiting for me. We walk back to the fire in silence.

Joanna and Nathaniel are anything but silent. They've spent the time that I was getting washed and dressed drinking that brown liquid, and they have become considerably merrier. They laugh at each other's lame jokes with hysterical whoops and keep filling up their bowls. Definitely alcoholic, that beverage. Perhaps I too should have some more. It might ease the pain in my arm and distract me from the drunken mating ritual that takes place in front of me. Or would my drunkenness only invite more Koeg? I can't risk that. I'll have to stay sober and watch helplessly while that blond hunk steadily charms his way into the heart of my intoxicated beloved.

Jago cast a brooding glance at the boozing couple, and after he and I both sat down he continues to stare at them, his frown becoming deeper with every giggle from the jolly duo. He clenches and unclenches his fists. I don't understand why he is getting so wound up, but when he resorts to tooth-gnashing I fear it's only a matter of time before he loses control and lashes out. While I don't enjoy Joanna and Nathaniel's continuous flirting, I think I'd enjoy a fistfight even less. Well, I wouldn't mind Nathaniel receiving a few well-placed blows, but not Joanna, so with Jago now about to start breathing fire I think I better try to distract him.

"You were going to tell me about the door," I say.

Jago grinds his teeth, which produces a scraping sound that gives me goose bumps.

"So what is the door made of?" I insist. "And how come you even got it? And the clothes, and the towels, and the bowls, and everything. There should be nothing here. It's supposed to be a Void. So how did you get all this stuff?"

Jago tears his gaze away from the drinking buddies and turns to me. "What?"

I repeat my questions. Jago casts a last dour glance at Joanna, who is now sitting on Nathaniel's lap, before he focuses on me.

"Imagination," he says. "This world, this realm, it was created by imagination. Regrettably, it was the imagination of a cruel man."

"Graham Gwithyas," I say.

"Indeed. You know of him? Are you one of the family?"

I shrug. I don't really feel like going into the exact details at the moment, and Jago appears to understand, because he doesn't pressure me.

"Graham could shape the forces of the hill," he says. "Like most of the Gwithyas family, I too possess that ability, albeit in a much weaker form. Since this realm has been created by thought it's possible to create objects within it, also by thought. That is what I do. That is how I fill the Void." He points at the floor in front of him. "What would you like?"

"Like?"

"Yes. What do you want me to imagine you up? It would have to be simple, something I know, something I can easily understand."

Right. He reckons he's going to do some magic for me then. And why not? It's not weirder than anything else that is going on here. So now all I need to do is decide what I would like. I change my sitting position, and a sharp pain tears through my arm and makes me gasp. That's the decision made, then.

"I'd like paracetamol," I say to Jago. He looks puzzled, so I explain, "Painkillers."

When his expression changes to concern, I lie, "I have a headache. I did not sleep well."

"Ah," says Jago, "You desire something to ease the pain." He frowns, tugs at his beard and shakes his head. "I can't do that. Liquor and opium do more harm than good. You are too young."

Liquor? Opium? What on Earth—I mean, what in the Void—is he on about?

"I don't want any hard drugs or alcohol," I tell him. "Just paracetamol or something equally harmless."

"Harmless pain medication?" asks Jago with a hint of excitement in his voice. "Such a thing exists?"

I'm starting to think that Jago may have been in the Void a little longer than he should have been. "Well, yeah," I reply. "Like Paracetamol or Ibuprofen, you know? Just over-the-counter stuff is all I want. Any brand will do."

Jago looks positively excited. His beard trembles. "How ingenious," he says. "Alas, I must apologise. I cannot make those, for I do not know what chemicals they contain."

I suppose that makes sense. It sucks though. I'd so looked forward to getting rid of this persistent nagging pain. I try not to show my disappointment and come up with another idea. If I can't be pain-free, I can at least try to get more comfortable.

"Could you do me a pillow?" I ask.

Jago shuts his eyes and the air in front of him starts to change. It turns first white, then solid, and then there is a large pillow on the ground. It's not your average pillow. It's a bit shiny and unusually square, but when I touch it, it's soft and bouncy. It's also very smooth, like everything else in here.

"Will that do?" asks Jago.

"Yes," I say, prodding a finger into the pillow. "That was incredible."

"It is not a real pillow," says Jago. "I am not powerful enough to create real objects. This matter is not fully formed. It is merely solidified magic."

I pick up my new bedding and press it against my chest. It feels real enough to me. And very soft.

On the other side of the fire the lively chatting has ceased and Joanna is glaring at us with fuzzy eyes.

"He magicked a pillow!" she squeals. "How diddee do that?"

"Oh, he dozzit all the time," says Nathaniel. "He diddiz drink too. Want some more?"

When Nathaniel raises a flask and readies himself to pour out more booze, Jago stands up and pulls the flask from Nathaniel's hand. "You've had enough."

Nathaniel attempts to grab the flask back but he misses. Jago holds it at a distance.

"No," he says. "It's time to cook anyway."

Nathaniel lets his hand drop, grins at Joanna and says, "I'll cook ya the most speciallesest meal ever, warrior princess." He gets up, staggers briefly and then ruffles Jago's hair. "C'mon then, you grumpy old git."

The two men walk away. Joanna giggles, gets up as well and shouts, "I'll help you, oh fearless knight!" She zigzags as she follows the others, and nearly trips over me.

"Get out of my way, you useless wuss!" she snarls, and she walks on, giggling and chatting loudly to Nathaniel.

I'm cold. Not all over. My cheeks are hot. I suspect they are also bright pink, but flushed cheeks don't do anything to warm a shivering body. I move closer to the fire. Joanna's irregular footsteps become quieter as she moves further away from me, and then fade altogether, but I still hear her voice. *Useless wuss.* My eyes sting and I have to swallow to stop myself from bursting out in tears. I put my freshly wizarded pillow on my legs to rest my sore arm on it, and I sit like that for a while, thinking about Joanna and Nathaniel, and then, without warning, about bog bodies on flowery sheets. No. I push the thought away. I need to concentrate on something else. *Useless wuss.* No, no, that won't do either. The fire. Fires are always mesmerising, and more importantly, distracting.

I stare into the flames. They appear to dance and play leap-frog together. They aren't quite normal flames, a bit too smooth and too bright around the edges, but they're warm and comforting nonetheless. Some even have faces.

Faces? I blink, once, twice, but they're still there. Little skulls of flame with fiery yellow eye-sockets.

"Surprise!"

The heat of the fire seeps through my eyes into my head, setting my brain ablaze while more and more skull-faces appear in the fire. They study me closely and chuckle.

"He's almost as orange as we are!"

"I wonder what he tastes like."

"Carrots of course!"

They laugh out loud at their own joke, spraying a shower of sparks over my hand onto the pillow, and I hastily pull my hand back. Hell, I'm getting so fed up with this. I'm too tired. And too depressed. I pick the pillow up and wave it at the fire. It flickers.

"Bugger off!" I say.

The flaming skulls gnash their fiery teeth. "Don't you like jokes? Surely you like games though. Play with us."

They lash out and my pillow catches fire. My pillow. My soft, comfy, magic pillow. My only true friend in this distorted hell-hole. I slap at the fabric with my good hand in an attempt to put out the fire, but I only succeed in singing my sleeve and arm-hairs while the pillow proceeds to burn in a spectacular fashion, with flames licking through its smooth whiteness, and I am forced to drop it. It burns ferociously at my feet. Bugger. If only I could do what Jago does then I'd turn the pillow's flames into water and throw it at those horrible little skulls.

A small orange spider scurries over the pillow, unfazed by the soaring fire.

"And why not?" it says. "All this is in the mind. Your mind."

A second spider tiptoes over my leg. "The Koeg are weak in this room," it says. "It's too full in here for them. They need emptiness."

"This is your chance, Gwithyas."

"Never mind them," hisses the fire. "Bugs are boring. Play with us! It'll be fun."

In front of my feet a trickle of smoke rises from the small pile of ashes that was once my pillow. I raise my head, look directly at the fire skulls, and this time it's me who does the tooth gnashing.

"I told you to bugger off!" I yell, and the smoke thickens into a transparent liquid that splashes over the flames in the hearth, extinguishing the fire and with it the sniggering Koeg. All that remains is a pile of scorched void-wood.

The two spiders hop onto it. "Well done!" they cheer, and then they are gone.

I squint at the damp wood in the hearth. I want my pillow back. I concentrate on the largest chunk. It shimmers and then smoothly shifts shape until it is a pillow. I pick the bedding up and place it on my lap to rest my sore arm on it again. I am a wizard now, how funny is that. I guess I shouldn't be surprised. Of course I can make these changes. The Void is anchored in my mind, because I am the Guardian. And the reason that I am the Guardian is that my father is dead. And the reason that my father is dead is that creatures from my mind killed him, which means I killed him. Somehow that thought makes my newly discovered ability less thrilling. In fact, I don't think I want to use it any more.

I stare into the empty fireplace until the others return.

CHAPTER 11
Dinner

"WHAT IN THE LORD'S NAME HAPPENED HERE?"

I jolt at the gruff shout. Jago, Nathaniel and Joanna are standing next to me. I must have dozed. Nathaniel, who appears to be sober again, is holding a small cauldron that has green fumes rising from it, and Joanna is carrying a collection of bowls and spoons. She too seems clear-headed. That drink can't have been very strong. Figures. Nothing here has substance to it, not even the alcohol.

Jago gestures at the empty fireplace. "How did that happen?"

I have no intention to explain what happened. They wouldn't believe me anyway. So I say, "Dunno. I was sleeping."

Jago grimaces and legs towards the hearth while Nathaniel places his cauldron on the floor and Joanna puts the bowls and spoons down. She nearly drops them because she keeps looking at me. Once the crockery is safely on the ground, Joanna points at my arm. "Did you burn yourself?"

I follow her gaze. My sleeve is frayed and scorched. "I must've come too near the fire," I say.

I don't think Joanna believes me, but before she can ask me anything else the fire comes back to life with a loud whoosh. Jago steps away from it.

"Sorted," he says. "The wood was damp."

"That's weird," says Joanna. "I mean, there's no water here or anything. Someone must have put the fire out on purpose. Or did it rain into the chimney or what?"

"We are in the Void," snorts Jago, "It does not rain here. Any water in this place comes from the well, and the well is a creation of my mind. I hope you are not implying that I extinguished the fire?"

"Of course not! I was just saying, I mean . . ." Joanna shuts her mouth, looking confused. Nathaniel touches her hand and gives Jago a glowering look.

"Let it rest," he says. "We should eat. We will be more able to solve mysteries with our stomachs full."

He kneels down next to the cauldron and starts ladling a gooey substance into the bowls. He serves us all before scooping out his own food and sitting down between Joanna and me.

"Bon appetit everyone," he says.

I study the contents of the bowl: a stodgy, unappealing green substance. I hold it under my nose. It smells spicy. I proceed to cautiously poke at the green stuff with one finger and it quivers as if it's trying to escape my touch. I'm not sure about this.

"Aren't you hungry?" asks Nathaniel.

"Not very," I say with a watchful eye on the food. "What is it anyway?"

"Just eat," says Nathaniel.

I prod at the food again. It wobbles. "Is this something that Jago has conjured up?"

"No," says Nathaniel. "Jago doesn't do food. Cooking is my skill. Eat it now and I'll reveal my culinary secrets later."

I don't really want to eat this vivacious blubber, but my stomach is empty and the Koeg like emptiness. I don't fancy the idea of a horde of blood-thirsty horrors settling in my digestive system, so I give in and start eating. It doesn't taste too bad, and as I continue to eat I'm actually starting to feel a little better. Before I know it my bowl is empty.

Nathaniel smiles at me. "Was it not too foul?"

"No," I say. "It was quite good, actually. So what was it?"

Nathaniel taps his fingers on his leg. "You might not want to know."

"Now I certainly do."

"All right then. It's squashed Koeg."

My oesophagus squirms and I can't stop myself from gagging. Nathaniel looks at me sideways, with a hint of a smile around his lips. "It's very nutritious," he says. "And it's the only thing those pests are good for. Besides, there isn't anything else to eat here. Jago hasn't been able to materialise anything even vaguely edible."

I have to swallow a couple of times to counteract my gag reflex before I can answer, "It's fine. Let's just not talk about it anymore. I wish I hadn't asked. Sorry."

He grins. "No need to apologise. Do you want more?"

I think this over. I still have no appetite, but I don't think my stomach is quite full yet, and I don't want to risk it going empty. I almost smile at the ridiculous notion of filling one's stomach with Koeg to keep out other Koeg. I run my finger over the bottom of my empty bowl. "You said there isn't anything else."

"There isn't."

"And I presume there won't be at a later stage."

"Very unlikely."

I take a deep breath. "Yes," I say, "I'd like some more, please."

During the remaining time of our supper we talk. Well, 'we' is an overstatement. Nathaniel, who seems blissfully unaffected by the uneasy atmosphere, talks a lot, as does Joanna. I think she's trying to impress Nathaniel. I can't see what is so impressive about fluttering eyelashes, squeaky giggles and pseudo-accidental brushes of fingertips against legs and shoulders. I might have felt different if all that had been directed at me, but now all I feel is disgust and irritation. So I sit, sulk and stay silent.

Jago is also silent. He stares into the fire while Nathaniel explains to us how to catch and prepare Koeg. Apparently all one has to do is take a stroll outside these rooms, and they will come.

"You only have a few moments," says Nathaniel. "The little ones always come first and if you're fast enough you can catch them before the big ones join them. You don't want the big ones, they're dangerous. Once you catch a Koeg, all you have to do is chop it in bits, stick it in the bag and bring it inside."

I reckon I'd make a lousy Koeg hunter, because I never get the small ones to come first, except maybe just now with the fire. I usually get Cecilia, and I got the DVD ape and the three-headed Koeg. I don't think any of those qualify as small ones.

"So chopping them up kills them?" enquires Joanna. "I mean, for definite? Like, they don't come back or reform or something? So why don't you run out of food then?"

"Chopping kills the Koeg," confirms Nathaniel. "It's the only thing that does, in fact. You need to really slash them to tiny bits though, or they regenerate. As for running out of Koeg . . ." His face darkens. "We have tried to kill them all. It didn't work. New ones keep appearing. It seems that Jago is not the only one in here who can shape the magic." He sighs. "But that's a different topic. Now where was I?"

He continues to describe the Koeg-preparation process, which involves slime, blood and body parts. I try hard to not listen, but Joanna seems spellbound. I don't think it matters to her what Nathaniel says, she just loves to hear his voice. Jago doesn't. At least not at the moment. He tells Nathaniel to stop spoiling everyone's appetite, and looks at me while he says that. Fair enough. I've not touched my second bowl of Koeg yet.

"Let's discuss more important matters," suggests Jago. "How did you two get in here?"

"It's his fault," says Joanna, pointing her spoon at me. "His father is the Guardian, and Zircon is supposed to follow in his Dad's footsteps, but he's more interested in fun and games. The Koeg were entering our world and he was sobbing like a baby while I was trying to fight them off. And then, instead of keeping them out of our world, he dragged us into theirs."

A heavy silence falls over the room. Joanna, Jago and

Nathaniel are all looking at me. My face goes hot. What Joanna said is true of course, kind of anyway. And it's worse too, but she doesn't know that. She doesn't know that I am responsible for my parents' deaths, and I want to keep it that way. Things are bad enough as they are. I turn my face away and stare at my feet. While I examine the holes in my socks, Nathaniel asks, "Did it hurt when the Koeg came?"

No one responds. When I look up I realise he was asking me.

"Did it?" he repeats.

"I… I did have a bit of a headache."

Joanna snorts. "Yes," she says, "that's his excuse for everything. And now we are stuck here, and we can't help his father to protect the world from a Koeg invasion. That was my task, you know. To help and protect the Guardian. I am his shield. Now the Guardian is on his own, and Zircon here has no idea what to do about it. All he does is whimper. And to think he is supposed to follow up his father; you'd expect him to be quite different, wouldn't you?"

"How different?" asks Nathaniel.

"Well," shrugs Joanna. "You'd think he'd be brave, selfless and strong. At least, that is how my uncle described the Guardian. So I guess I'd imagined him to be more like . . ." She glances at Nathaniel.

"Like me?" he asks.

Joanna's cheeks darken. "Yes."

"You don't know if I'm brave and selfless," points Nathaniel out. "You have only just met me. Things aren't always what they seem."

"He *is* brave and selfless," interrupts Jago. "Nathaniel was also supposed to become a Guardian, but he never got the chance. He was pulled through the doorway trying to protect his younger siblings."

Joanna glances at Nathaniel. Her eyes are shining. "Is that so?"

Nathaniel nods. "It was a long time ago. I was a young man and my mother was the Guardian. I was the eldest of nine siblings, some of them still very small. One of my sisters . . ." He stops speaking and sits still, biting his lower lip as if he's about to cry. Joanna has her wide-open, moist eyes firmly fixed on Nathaniel's tormented face. Her hand is moving towards him as if she wants to touch him but doesn't dare. It's just like one of those sentimental romantic dramas Mum likes—liked. I shudder, push away all thoughts of my family and face away from the mushy couple, at Jago. His eyebrows resemble a couple of obese caterpillars, but I can't tell if he's looking at Nathaniel or at Joanna. Nathaniel takes a deep breath and continues his story.

"My mother was in the tower with Nanny when the Koeg came down the chimney, grasping at my little siblings. I couldn't stop it. The children were crying, terrified, and I knew all hell would break loose. Literally, because back then I thought this place was hell. I did the only thing I could think of. I went through and I shut the door."

He stops talking and stares into his bowl. Joanna can't control herself any longer. She places her hand on his arm. "That must've been so hard," she says in a sugar-coated voice. "Such a brave, selfless thing to do. You're a hero, Nathaniel. A true Guardian."

She squeezes his arm and smiles at him, a faint, trembling little smile. My insides are also faint and trembling. I feel sick. Jago snorts heavily, like an angry bull. His eyebrows are so low that they almost obscure his dark glare. He scrapes some dust from the floor and tosses it into the fire, just barely missing Joanna and Nathaniel. He collects more dust in his hand, but before he can throw it I ask him, "And you? How did you get here?"

He looks at me, blinks, opens his hand so the dust falls out, and says, "Back in the beginning we didn't know. Errors were made. My elder sister was the Guardian, and I was assisting her. We did not perform the ritual correctly. She was knocked unconscious and I fell through."

"In the beginning?" asks Joanna. "When was that then?"

"1640," says Jago. "Angus Gwithyas was my father."

Both Joanna and I are lost for words. I am the first one to

come to my senses. Kind of, anyway. "You look good for your age," I say.

Jago scowls, but Nathaniel chuckles and pats me on the shoulder.

"Well said," he says, "Poor old Jago could do with a compliment. The presence of this gorgeous maiden here is wrecking his confidence."

"I don't understand," stammers the maiden in question. "How is that possible? And . . ." she glances suspiciously at Nathaniel, "how old are you?"

"How old?" he repeats. "That's a good question. Truth is, I cannot tell. I was born in 1757, but in here time is different. When I arrived Jago swore he'd only been here for three weeks, but now we are not certain. Jago's watch stopped working a while ago. I'd estimate we've been here about two or three years. Maybe four. What year are you from?"

"2016," I say. "Which is more than two and a half centuries after you came here, and yet you are still alive. So there is no consistent linear relationship between the passage of time in the real world and the Void."

Nathaniel raises his eyebrows. "I have no idea what that means," he says. "But I'm sure that Jago does."

"Yes," says Jago. "And he is right. The passage of time here is random. Just like everything else."

"You don't talk old-fashioned," I say. "If you are from that long ago you should sound very different from us, but you don't."

"I have no explanation for that," says Jago.

I think that maybe I have. I remember the large three-headed Koeg, and how I couldn't hear what it said, yet I knew what it meant. Perhaps this is the same. Or perhaps I am clutching at straws here. It's still possible that I am hallucinating all this. That would explain why I can understand everyone: they are all effectively me. I examine them. Gloomy, serious Jago; handsome, chatty Nathaniel; and brave, gorgeous Joanna, who is now smiling at Nathaniel and pouting her lips—the first time I've seen her do that. They are so different from me. How could they be my hallucinations? And then there is my arm, which is hot and throbs violently. That pain feels pretty real. I fold back my sleeve and expose a swollen, shiny, inflamed hand. Great. It's infected. The Koeg only know with what. Does this place contain the same microbes as the normal world? Another thought strikes me: if this is a genuine infection, I cannot possibly be in a psychiatric hospital. No hospital would allow a mentally ill patient to get this badly injured and then neglect to treat the wounds. So the Void and everything else cannot be a hallucination. It has to be real. The Koeg have to be real. Which means that every single horror that has happened lately has to be real. I knew that of course. I just didn't want it to be true. I pull my sleeve back over my throbbing hand and shut my eyes.

I don't know how long I've been sitting like that, but I become a little drowsy, and only come back to my senses when a man's voice asks, "Are you all right?"

I think it's Nathaniel. He is patting my cheek. "Zircon?" He sounds urgent. Perhaps I should say something back.

"Yes?" I say. "Sorry. I was . . . I must have . . ." I stop speaking, not sure what I was going to say. Nathaniel gives me an inquisitive look. His hands are resting on my shoulders, which is oddly reassuring. "What's the matter, Zircon?"

"I-I'm tired," I lie.

Nathaniel cocks his head. "Tired?"

"Yes," I say. "It's been a long day."

"Of course," says Nathaniel. "It has been. You must be exhausted. I'll prepare a bed for you." He gives my shoulders a soft squeeze before he leaves.

I don't know what to make of him. I want to be angry with him because Joanna likes him so much, but it's hard because he is so kind to me. From across the fire, Jago gives me one of his brooding gazes.

"Are you the Guardian?" he asks.

Joanna replies before I can utter a single word. "I told you that he isn't," she says. "His father is still alive."

"You can't be certain of that," argues Jago. "For all we know sixty years have passed in the manor since you arrived here and the man has died of old age."

I open my mouth to tell him that my father will never die of old age, that he will never even experience old age, but then I remember that it's my fault that he won't, so I don't say anything and stick a spoonful of Koeg puree into my open mouth instead. Joanna points at me. "So he could be the Guardian?" she asks Jago.

Jago shakes his head. "Probably not. If his father was still alive when you two went through the doorway, that would mean the doorway would have to be transferred through itself, from Zircon's father in the real world to his son in this place. That is not possible."

"So Zircon will never become the Guardian?" inquires Joanna.

Her voice is sharp, and when Jago says, "Like I said: that is not possible," she slams her bowl on the floor, leaps up and walks over to me.

"Nicely done, goggles," she snarls. "Not only did you drag us in here, no, you also made sure that you will never be able to open the doorway so we are stuck here for eternity."

She sounds weird and kind of shaky. I look up at her. Big, round tears are rolling from her gorgeous almond eyes down her velvety brown cheeks.

"It may make no difference to you," she sniffles. "But I had a life! I had my uncle, I had friends, I was going to university next year. And now I have to exist in this empty hell. All because you are an irresponsible coward, and a complete and utter failure. I hate you."

She turns on her heels and walks to the wall opposite of me. She presses her hands against it and lets her head hang between her stretched arms. Her shoulders shake to the rhythm of her desperate sobs. No one speaks.

The spoonful of Koeg puree stays in my mouth. I can't swallow it. I have the faint notion that I should object, be assertive, tell them it's not true, that my father is dead and that I am the Guardian, so I can open the doorway. But that would mean admitting that I am a murderer, and I don't think they would like me a lot if they knew that. Plus, although I *should* be able to open the doorway, I haven't a clue how to do that. So I just sit daftly with my mouth full of unchewed Koeg.

Then Nathaniel appears. Of course he does. Like a true superhero, always in the right place at the right time. He knows exactly what to do as well. He walks over to Joanna, takes her hand in his and quietly talks to her. She replies in short blubbery stutters. He strokes her hair. His elegant fingers brush through her cascading locks, making them bounce like the dense foliage of oak trees in a summer storm. I am so mesmerised by this sight that I don't notice that Jago has come to sit next to me. He puts his arm over my shoulders and holds a bowl under my mouth.

"Spit it out," he says. "You'll choke."

I open my mouth and the squashed Koeg dribbles over my lower lip and my chin into the bowl. My stomach leaps at the opportunity, cramps up and regurgitates all its contents into the bowl, and on the floor, and over Jago's hand and sleeve. Jago doesn't even flinch. Instead, he rubs my back. "I think you need to go to bed," he says.

That sounds like a good idea. I ought to get up first, of course. I mean, I need to walk over to the bed before I can lie down in it. That's a problem because it seems that I can't remember how to walk. Or even how to stand up.

"Come on," says Nathaniel. No idea how he suddenly got here. He slides his arms under my knees and my shoulders, and I start to float. And then I'm in the bed. I don't sleep, at least I don't think I do. I just lie there with my eyes shut while somebody is wiping my face with a damp cloth.

"This will hurt." I think it's Jago who said that. Why would he want to hurt me? Is he a Koeg as well? He touches my arm and it stings. I try to pull it away.

"Sorry, lad," says Jago, and then he says a lot more but I can't make out the words. My arm keeps stinging, but it's not too bad, and I'm too tired to care anyway.

The others are talking to each other in meaningless jumbled syllables. My arm doesn't sting any more, but it now feels strangely stiff. Someone says my name. I open my eyes and see Joanna. She's frowning and her eyes are red, with swollen eyelids. I wonder if she has a boyfriend back home. Had. If she did, she'll never see him again. Maybe he has married, become a father, a grandfather even. Or maybe he's still in college now, wondering why Joanna isn't there too. He doesn't know that she is lost in an evil Void with loads of monsters, with no way out. He doesn't know that some stupid, good-for-nothing geek has ruined her life.

"I'm sorry," I whisper. "I'm so sorry."

Her frown disappears. "Go to sleep," she says.

I close my eyes.

Spiders scuttle over my face, up and down.

"You need to talk to the others," says one of them.

"They need to know that you are the Guardian."

"Especially your shield. You need her. Stay close to her. She will protect you."

"She hates me," I object. "And if I tell them that I am the Guardian they will figure out that my father is dead and they will know that I am responsible. They will know that I am a murderer."

"You are rambling," say the spiders. "Nobody thinks you are a killer."

The tiny feet change into fingers that softly stroke my face and my hands.

"He is very ill," says Opal, because it are her fingers that brush over my cheek.

"He is not thinking straight," agrees Amethyst.

She strokes my arm and I realise that it's bandaged. Did Jago do that?

"You need to rest," says Opal, and her fingers touch my eyelids. I close them.

"Sleep now, brave brother."

"We will give you sweet dreams."

CHAPTER 12
Fever

I'VE NEVER CAUGHT OPAL OR AMETHYST FIBBING, AND THEY certainly didn't this time. My dreams are pleasant. There is the fat lazy cat we had when I was little, who would roll over for a belly rub. There is the cherry tree that we'd climb on hot summer days to eat the sweet cherries. There is the time my sisters and I performed a self-written play for our parents and my mother cheered and my father almost smiled. When the play ends Amethyst takes my hand to guide me into the next stage of sleep. "You have to tell them, Zircon," she whispers.

I will. I will tell Joanna, and she'll tell Nathaniel and Jago. Oh, I will. But not now. Now I will enjoy a deep, dreamless sleep.

"Hello Gwithyas!"

Ah blast. Not dreamless after all. Why won't they just leave me alone?

"You know why," says Cecilia. "We want to play. You like cats, don't you?"

She has a pet with her, lucky girl. "This is my cat," she claims. "Just like the one you used to have."

She's wrong there. My cat had a head, and it didn't have slimy hairless skin. It didn't wail like a banshee with a bad bout of pneumonia either. Cecilia's pet is most certainly not a cat.

"I told you that I don't like your games," I tell Cecilia, "and I don't like your pet either."

She sulks. Her pet rots away like one of those time-lapse films of natural processes that normally take days.

Cecilia taps her chin. "I think I know what your problem is," she says. "It's that fluffy girl, isn't it?"

I don't answer. I don't want to discuss Joanna with this atrocious monster.

"You are stupid," says Cecilia. "She doesn't like you. She likes Nathaniel. Handsome, heroic, goody-two-shoes Nathaniel. He's a twat." She spits, and her saliva burns a hole in my blanket. "But not to worry, Gwithyas. You can have another girlfriend."

A round-bosomed, long-legged teenager pops up from behind Cecilia, giggling frantically.

"Will she do?" asks Cecilia.

I examine the curvy new arrival, especially the entrancing way her voluptuous bosom rises and falls with every breath. I need a breath myself, and a deep one too. It doesn't help. I can't keep my eyes off the girl. I thought women like that only existed in over-the-top action films and car commercials.

I lick my lips. I shouldn't really. I'm supposed to marry Joanna. But she made it clear that she doesn't want me, and even if she would, she deserves something better than an insane murderer with lousy social skills. So after another close observation of the Koeg-girl's conspicuous physical assets I say, "Yeah, she's fine."

The girl claps her hands. Her lips swell up in a blood-red pout. "Kiss me, Gwithyas." The lips inflate like party balloons until they touch mine. They are slimy and they burn. "Kissie kiss kiss!"

I recoil and the girl evaporates in a cloud of giggles.

"Didn't you like her after all?" enquires Cecilia. "Never mind. You won't need a girlfriend when you're dead. Not long now, Gwithyas. You're getting weaker. Your body is ailing, your mind is muddled and your emotions are down."

She shows me her clenched fist, a proper little girl's fist, small and pink. She opens it. There, in her chubby palm, lies a shiny orange stone. A zircon. My zircon.

"See this? This is the link. Remember? Your uncle told you, didn't he? Very powerful, this little stone. And now I have it."

She tosses the stone in the air and catches it with her other hand. "This is a good time for us Koeg. The witch is dead, and the last Gwithyas—that would be you—is a weakling and a cowardly fool. We shall crush your will, and once you give in nothing will stand between us and the force from which we rose. We shall be able to control ourselves, and we shall open the door. Easy peasy."

I launch myself from my bed and dash forward in an attempt to snatch the gem off her. Pointless of course. Cecilia simply zaps herself a few feet further back.

"You are so useless," she scowls. "You're making it too easy. I like a bit of a chase. Let's make a deal." She bends over and dangles the zircon in front of my face.

"I shall hide this. I shall give you a chance to get it back just so I can have some fun. It is hidden in the bedroom, Gwithyas. Up the stairs. Come and get it if you want but don't let the others know. If you do we will tell them all about you. We will tell them how you killed your mummy and daddy."

And then she fades, leaving behind only the orange glow of the zircon.

"Give it back!" I shout. "It's not yours. Give it back!"

"Calm down Zircon! Geez."

I jerk up. I'm in my Void-bed and Joanna is trying to take one of my blankets.

"The fire went out," she explains. "I got cold. So since you have three blankets, I thought you could miss one. Apparently you don't agree."

"No," I say. "I'm sorry. It's fine. I didn't mean the blanket. I was dreaming."

It's a blooming great effort to say such a long sentence. It leaves me out of breath.

Joanna's expression softens. "You are really quite ill, aren't you?" she asks.

"You can have the blanket," I say.

"That's not what I asked."

Oh no. She asked if I was ill. I wrecked her life. Why would she care? I shake my head.

"You're not ill?"

"No. Have the blanket."

Joanna sighs. "I don't understand you," she says. "I really don't."

And then she's gone, without taking a blanket. I'm not sure where she went. I can't see her. I hear footsteps, probably hers. So she's still here, suffering the consequences of my stupidity. Of course she is. It's my fault, so I should take responsibility, not just for Joanna's situation. For everything. If Cecilia told me the truth, the Koeg will invade our world soon, even though I'm in the Void. I need to stop them. And she gave me a chance. A chance to get the stone back, and then they can't go through to my world any more. Upstairs, she said. The stairs are at the end of the corridor. I don't want to go wading over that living floor again but I have no choice.

What am I thinking? Stairs at the end of the corridor? This isn't my home! The stairs and the gem could be anywhere. Unless… I open my eyes and look at the white walls. They're alien, yet so familiar. This room with the fireplace, the small empty entrance hall that should have been full, and even that weird kitchen. I remember now. The black tiles. The enormous fireplace. It is indeed a kitchen. The old kitchen from the manor. So this is my home, which means that there will be stairs at the end of the corridor. I push the blankets away. They refuse to go.

"What are you doing?"

Joanna again. I need to tell her that I am going to get the gem back, so I need to get up, but the blankets are too heavy. Only I can't speak.

"Zircon?" Her hand touches my forehead. Her fingers softly stroke my hair. I really must be dreaming.

"You're burning up," says Joanna. "I'm going to get Jago. I'll be back in a second."

I think she went, but I'm not sure. Uncle Ronald is here now. So he hasn't melted after all. I'm not sure how he got in the Void, though. Nothing is clear any more. Uncle Ronald looks at me disapprovingly.

"To a Gwithyas the goal is always clear," he says solemnly. "Just like it is to you. You are just denying what you know."

"But I'm sick."

Uncle Ronald shakes his head. "A weak excuse from a weak man. Your task is clear. What significance has your physical discomfort compared to the safety of humanity?"

"I can't get up!"

Uncle Ronald grabs my hands, drags me from the bed and puts me on my feet. I cry out as pain soars through my arm and my head.

"You're an embarrassment!" bellows Uncle Ronald. "You are not worthy the title of Guardian."

His face is so close to mine that I can smell him, and the smell reminds me of that time I found a decomposing rabbit in the shed.

"Hurry!" he hisses. "It's not too late. Get the gem."

Oh yes. Get the gem. That's what I need to do.

"Hurry!" insists my uncle.

I walk through the room and into the empty white entrance hall. My feet feel as if they're made of iron: heavy and inflexible, while my legs are like rubber. I want to stop walking. Perhaps the zircon is here in the little hall, and I don't have to go further. I search the floor and the walls. It doesn't take long. At home the hall is stacked full of stuff, but here it's as empty as can be. Perhaps Dad had a good reason to hoard so much rubbish. Perhaps Jago and Nathaniel also have a reason for filling up their living quarters with pointless objects. Fill up the Void to keep out the Koeg. Does emptiness create insanity? I never heard or read that before, but it might well be true. Or otherwise, insanity creates emptiness.

"Hurry!" Uncle Ronald's voice has become a barely audible whisper, and when I turn to face him he's not there. Never mind. I know what to do. I get onto my knees and my right hand and crawl through the arch.

I dreaded having to deal with the living floor again, but when I put my hand down in the corridor there is only solid stone. A perfectly ordinary floor. It doesn't breathe or pulsate, and when I stand my feet do not sink into it. Old tiles, like back home. In fact, this entire corridor is a duplicate from the one in my house, complete with the rickety staircase at the end. The only difference is that at home the corridor's walls are full of framed pictures, while here there is only one. It's one that I've never seen in the real manor: a photograph of my father and mother. They're smiling. More grinning actually, and such wide grins too. I look closer, with my glasses a finger-width away from the image. They're not smiling at all. Their teeth are showing because their dehydrated lips are withdrawn from their gums. What I thought were smiles are in fact the death-grimaces of bog bodies. I stagger back and the photo disappears. Perhaps I only imagined it.

I make my way to the stairs. They too are just like the ones back home: plain and dark with woodworm holes. I place an unsteady foot on the first step and start to climb. I don't think I'll make it all the way up, but to my surprise it takes only three steps to get to the upstairs corridor, where Uncle Ronald is waiting for me.

"I told you to hang on to that stone," he sneers. "You messed up!"

"I'm sorry," I say. "I'm trying to put it right."

"My brother died," sulks my uncle. "You won't put that right, now will you? I can't believe Paul fathered such a useless brat. The world is doomed."

"I'll find it!" I assure him. "I'll find the zircon and I'll keep the doorway shut."

Uncle Ronald snorts and opens a door to a dark room. "I hope so. The stone is in here."

I enter the room and the door slams shut behind me. It's pitch dark in here. I take a moment to get my bearings and then I slowly move forward over fluffy floor coverings, step by step, my hand stretched out, until my shin bumps against something hard. I move my fingers down to feel it. It's wood, the side of a wooden bed, and when I feel further I recognise the carved decorations in the wood, the soft foam of the mattress and the stiff cotton of the sheets. This is my parents' bed. This is where they died. They might still be in there.

I dare not feel for them and I certainly don't want to collapse on top of them and cause their dry corpses to crumble under my weight. But I'm tired and my legs hurt, so I sit down on the edge of the mattress. Rest a little, only briefly. It turns out that I am not permitted such luxuries. As soon as my behind touches the sheets Cecilia pops up. Apparently she needs no light to be visible. She is younger than ever: four at most. Her eyes are blue and wide and her lips are like tiny rosebuds, and they tremble when she squeaks, "I want to go home."

She points a chubby toddler-finger to a door. It's a massive oak thing with wild engravings, just like the front door of the Gwithyas manor.

"I used to live in the manor too," says Cecilia. "I have been in here for so long now. I don't like it anymore." A single teardrop rolls over her pink cheek. "Please, Gwithyas, open it. Let us go home. Please."

I want nothing more. I walk to the door. Cecilia darts ahead and waits next to the door. I place my hand on the doorknob and push it down. The door clicks and opens a tiny fraction.

Then my sisters appear behind Cecilia, hand in hand, and they are shaking their heads.

"You cannot let them through."

Cecilia turns on the heels of her shiny white shoes. "Keep out of this!" she snarls at my sisters, but they ignore her.

"Remember the skulls," says Opal.

"And Mum and Dad," adds Amethyst.

I don't want to think about that. I really don't. I place my hands over my ears. Opal and Amethyst are undeterred. Their voices are only slightly dimmed by my hands.

"If you open the door, people will die."

"Innocent people."

"You have a responsibility, Zircon. Shut that door."

They are right. Of course they are right. I pull the door shut. Cecilia scowls.

"All right," she says. "If that's the way you want it. I gave you a chance to cooperate. You can't say I didn't try."

She sticks her thumb in her mouth and twists her hair. No, that's wrong. Her hair is twisting itself over her arm. Then the golden locks turn into slimy tentacles that lash out at my sisters. The girls evaporate in a puff of orange smoke. I call their names. Cecilia laughs. "They're gone. You are alone. I lured you here because you are weak on your own. Now we shall torture you until you give up. Stupid boy."

"I'm not stupid!" I say. "I'll get the gem back. And I'm not alone. I have help!"

I look around. The room is still as dark as a broken computer monitor, but the Koeg that are starting to appear everywhere are clearly visible. There are quite a few now, all shapes and sizes, all squirming and wailing. There is also my uncle. I point at him. "There. He's my uncle, my father's brother. He will help me. Tell them, Uncle. We will get the gem back and everyone will be safe."

Uncle Ronald clears his throat before he speaks. He has a lot of clearing to do. His hand, and then his entire arm dives down his mouth and neck and comes back out, pulling along a bloody trail of intestines and other organs. Uncle Ronald tosses them at my feet.

"We tricked you," he gargles. "You are so weak. You don't stand a chance on your own. Now we rip you to shreds, dearest nephew, and we will keep ripping until you can't hold yourself together any longer. Then, the magic of the Gwithyas will be ours."

"You're my uncle!" I shout. "You were helping me."

He laughs, which sounds as if someone is draining a bath full of slugs.

"There is a reason good old Paul never mentioned me. I'm quite an embarrassment to him. Like sweet little Cecilia here is to her brother."

Bits of flesh spray from his mouth as his laughter collapses into slimy gasps. One bloody chunk lands on my shoulder. I try to brush it off, but it's stuck. It turns into a long thin Koeg that wraps itself around my neck. Uncle Ronald roars with guttural laughter. I can't breathe.

Cecilia raises her arms. "Get him!" she shouts.

The Koeg howl with joy as they grab me, pull and twist my limbs, tear at my skin. I think perhaps I am howling as well, but I can't discriminate my own voice from the thousands that surround me. I still can't breathe. I'm seeing stars now. Not long before I will pass out. Not long at all, and then it will be over. Cecilia whispers into my ear.

"No, Gwithyas. We cannot grant you such an easy way out. You first need to lose your mind."

The strangler Koeg lets go of my neck, but I'm not even relieved. I'd rather pass out. I try to hold my breath, but my body won't let me and forces me to suck in air that tastes of sulphur. Cecilia presses something into the palm of my open hand: the zircon. I can't understand why she'd give it to me. Must be another trick. Not that it matters. If I can get a hold of the stone I should be able to make it all good. I try to grab the gem, but I'm too weak and I can barely move my fingers.

Cecilia laughs. "Just give up, Gwithyas! There is nothing left to fight for. No one cares, no one is helping you. For you, there is only pain. Give up."

The Koeg keep attacking me, battering my body. I hear my bones snap. Worse, I feel it. A warm liquid wells up in my mouth. Blood. I stop struggling. I can't do this anymore. I don't really care anymore either. Cecilia strokes my bloodied cheek.

"That's it, Gwithyas," she says. "Give up, end the struggle. Hand the control to me."

The zircon in my hand goes cold. The Koeg shriek with delight, slashing more claws and teeth into me.

"That's it!" pants Cecilia. "Go on, Gwithyas. Do it!"

And then the sound of cheering Koeg is shattered by a single berserk yowl. *"Leave him alone!"*

That's Joanna, yelling at the top of her voice. Her sword pierces the dark and Cecilia is gone. Now, with nothing to hold me up, I collapse on the floor. I can't move and I can't see. I can feel though, and I feel that the Koeg are still attacking me, still biting and clawing at me wherever they can. I can hear, too. I hear Joanna shout, "Hang on Zircon! I'll get you out! Hang on!"

Her sword sweeps right past me, slashing several Koeg away. But it's too late. I try to say sorry to Joanna, but my jaw is broken so I cannot speak. Then I die.

CHAPTER 13
Dead

DEATH IS NOT WHAT I EXPECTED. INSTEAD OF LYING ON MY back with my hands neatly folded on my chest I am standing on a black tiled floor, facing a stone wall with metal hooks attached to it. I recognise that wall. I'm in the old kitchen again. So I'm not dead. I am home.

I smile. It all makes sense now. When I went into the old kitchen I must've slipped, hit my head and passed out, and everything about the Koeg and the Void and my parents' deaths was just a dream. All I have to do now is go back upstairs and . . .

My joyful thoughts are cut short when I spot a boy running towards me. He's about ten, bare-footed, and his face is covered in blood. He doesn't slow down as he approaches me and it's too late to step out of his path. I brace myself for a collision, but it doesn't happen. The boy runs straight through me. Then he's gone. I'm so shocked that I just stand there, motionless, wondering what the hell just happened.

"Please…"

I turn my head to see who said that. It's a woman. She is standing next to me, so close that our shoulders touch. Her dark hair is arranged in an intricate bun and she's wearing a long, high-collared dress. She looks as if she is about to take part in a costume drama. If that were true, if this were a play, she'd be a damn good actress. The tears that roll over her cheeks strike me as completely genuine. Her lips are moving, forming the same word over and over: "*please, please, please . . .*"

She raises her hand, and so do I. Not because I intended to do so, but because my fingers are tightly folded around the woman's wrist and I am unable to let go. The woman doesn't seem to be aware of this. She opens her hand and calls out, "Graham! *Please*!"

Graham? I follow the woman's gaze to a tall man with ginger sideburns who is standing in front of the fireplace with his arms in the air. A whirlwind of distorted shapes twirls around his head. Koeg. The boy who just ran through me is also there, cowering against the wall, next to a teenage girl with a bonnet.

As I am watching, one of the Koeg breaks away from the whirlwind and launches itself at the girl. She cries out in terror, but not for long. One slash of the Koeg's long claws and her severed head rolls over the floor, squirting blood. It comes to a halt in front of my feet, face up. I look into the girls' green eyes. They are glassy and dead and yet, somehow, they look at me accusingly. The woman whose wrist I'm holding cries out even louder than the girl had done.

"Graham! Stop it! Please. *Please*!"

This time the man hears her. He turns around. His eyes are wild, and he is grinning like a maniac. A fanged Koeg hurls itself via his arm towards the woman and me. I duck. The woman gasps. From ahead of us a deep, raw voice howls: "*Sophie!*"

The woman—Sophie I presume—collapses. Because my hand is still stuck to her wrist I tumble down along with her. I land on my stomach with my hand trapped between the cold stone floor and Sophie's limp arm. I try to free my hand, but my fingers won't move. Something pinches into my palm. I turn my head to see what it is. Between my thumb and index finger there's a faint orange glimmer. The zircon. It is set in the silver bracelet around Sophie's wrist. I can't understand how this happened, let alone what it means, but this is not the time and place to try and figure it out.

Graham has ceased his mad wizard performance and falls on his knees next to Sophie, and very nearly on top of me. He strokes Sophie's blood-drenched hair while whispering her name. He smells of sweat and sulphur. I guess that's what happens if you insist on meddling with old magic and Koeg. The Koeg are still twirling and bouncing around Graham and cheer when he starts to groan like an injured grizzly bear.

There is a shout from further away, and then the sound of someone running towards us. I fidget and wriggle until I can turn my head far enough to see that it's a young man who looks a lot like Graham, but minus the gingerness. Must be Angus Gwithyas, Graham's son. He falls on his knees next to Sophie's body, touches her, whimpers, and then turns to Graham, his face twisted with pure hatred.

"She's dead!" he shouts. "You killed her! *You killed her!*"

Behind the young man a second figure appears, a tall, slender woman with familiar misty blue eyes. Nanny. Not the demon-Nanny with the split purple tongue, but the other, sweet Nanny, the one I met just after I performed the last ritual. Only she's a lot younger now. And not dead, of course. She places her hand on Angus' shoulder.

"Now is not the time to grieve," she says. "We have to act."

I couldn't agree with her more. In the time it has taken young Angus to come here and display his despair, the kitchen has filled up with more Koeg than I've ever seen. Nanny says to Graham, "Is this what you wanted?" but Graham is too busy moaning to reply.

"Graham Gwithyas!" bellows Nanny. "You need to stop this. They took your wife. It is only a matter of moments before they take your son. Stop it!"

Now Graham raises his head. He has his back to me so I cannot see his face, but I can just see his right sideburn tremble when he replies, "I can't. I don't know how."

The Koeg respond to his words with hysterical laughter. They twist through the kitchen more violently than before, and occasionally hurl themselves at Nanny and Angus. Fortunately they don't take any notice of me. Nanny slaps at the Koeg as if they were a bunch of flies and points a finger in Graham's direction.

"Shut the door. You have to shut the door."

It's almost as if she is speaking to me, but it's Graham who reacts. He throws his ginger head back and howls, *"I don't know how!"*

A large Koeg launches itself at Angus, who only just manages to duck deep enough to evade it. Nanny grabs Graham's hand and says, "The bracelet! Hold the bracelet!"

Graham twists on his knees and with his free hand he grabs Sophie's wrist. His hand closes over mine, pressing my skin further onto the sharp edge of the zircon. A tiny trickle of blood appears between my palm and Sophie's dead flesh, and then Graham sees me. His eyes grow wide.

"Who . . ." he starts, but his words are drowned by the furious screeches of the Koeg. They leave Angus alone and all attack Nanny, who is standing between the two men, holding one hand of each. She opens her mouth. I can barely distinguish her voice in the cacophony of Koeg-noises, but I recognise her words: *"Gwitha sallow!"*

I die again.

This time death is appropriately dark and silent. I'm still not lying down like a proper corpse though. I'm kneeling on a rough wooden floor. I'm cold. I shiver and rub my upper arms with my fists, but I don't get any warmer. I'm starting to worry that I'll have to spend the ever-after wishing for a fleece jumper when someone calls my name.

"Zircon!"

An orange spark emerges in the dark, and then a second one. My two orange spider companions are shimmering in front of me. Only they're not spiders. How come I never noticed that before? They are nothing but bright orange lights.

"You should not be here!" they say.

Some welcome. And I don't even know where 'here' is. Could be heaven, or hell, or Valhalla, or wherever departed souls end up these days. I had always assumed we simply cease to exist after we die, but apparently I was wrong.

"Where am I?" I ask.

"Don't you recognise it?"

The darkness dissipates, making place for a familiar brick wall. I'm in Nanny's tower. The spider-lights sizzle around my head.

"Why are you here?" they ask.

"Beats me," I say. "I thought I was dead."

The lights flicker and disappear. In their place there are now my sisters, Opal and Amethyst, but they look weird. Or actually, they don't. For the first time ever they look normal. Amethyst has rosy cheeks, and her eyes aren't beady and black but large and hazel. Behind her Opal's brown curls pop up, bouncing lively over her glinting green eyes.

"What the hell?" I mutter.

"Hi," says Amethyst.

I don't say hi back. I stand up and touch her hair. It's soft and not in the least dry. This isn't right. I back away.

"Why do you look like that?" I ask. "And how come I still know who you are?"

Opal cocks her head. "This is what we used to look like, Zircon. You recognise us because you know our souls."

"Souls?"

"The orange lights," explains Amethyst. "Those are our souls."

I smirk. Typical. My sisters would believe anything as long as it's weird.

"That's rubbish," I say. "You've been playing with your Ouija board too much. Why would your souls be orange? And why would you two flutter about in soul-shape anyway?"

"Souls don't actually look like anything," says Opal. "It's your mind that creates their appearance. And you happen to have a thing for shiny orange objects."

Amethyst adds, "We take that shape because our souls are all that is left of us. We are dead, Zircon."

"Dead?"

I pore over her face. Her eyes are wide, shiny and moist. She looks more alive than she has ever done.

"Rubbish," I say.

"We died a long time ago," says Opal. "Long before you were born. We are not actually your sisters."

Not my sisters? I laugh. A weird, high-pitched laugh. Embarrassing, but I can't stop it.

"You're m-mad," I stammer. "Totally mad. Of course you are my sisters. You are my family. You two and I are the only ones left."

Opal shakes her head. Her curls brush over the fair skin of her forehead. "I'm sorry, Zircon. We were siblings to two of your ancestors. We were born into the Gwithyas family. We used to live in the manor until we fell through the doorway, like Nathaniel and Jago did. Only unlike them, we didn't survive. We died in the Void."

"Our souls could not pass," says Amethyst. "When you die in the Void, you remain there. In fact, you end up exactly here, in this room."

"So you see," continues Opal. "You too must be dead or dying, or you wouldn't be here. But that is not possible. You are the Gwithyas. The Void is in you, so you cannot die in the Void."

"Oh yes he can!"

The snarling voice comes from straight ahead. When I looked the first time there was only a wall, but now Nanny is there, seated in her trusty rocking chair. She's not in her demon shape, and her misty blue eyes are fixed on me, but they are not sweet and loving like on the day she died. More like menacing. It seems Nanny is cross with me.

"The Gwithyas can die in the Void if he chooses to," she

says. "And you, Peregrine Zircon, you chose to die, because you are weak and cowardly. You failed. The world is doomed and it's your fault."

Amethyst places her arm over my shoulders. "That is hardly fair, Nanny," she says. "He tried. He's just a boy, and he was being tortured."

Nanny scowls. Her long fingers pluck tiny fuzz balls from the fabric of her dress. It's the dress she was wearing when she was young in the kitchen.

"Tried?" she sneers. "Do you call it trying when he hands his powers to the Koeg? Do you? Because that is what he did. The last gem, the only remaining link between the powers of the Gwithyas, Graham's mind, and my spells: he gave it to that wretched child. He gave it to Cecilia. He gave it willingly."

She points a crooked finger at me. "And now you are dead. The last Guardian, the only one who stood between the Koeg and their goal."

She glares at me, her cloudy eyes full of rage. I prepare myself for more allegations, but Nanny only utters an exasperated sigh and curls back into her chair. Her head slumps forward so her hair falls over her face like a white veil as the feisty, angry witch collapses into a tired old woman. She starts to pull fuzz from her dress again, more frantically now, and she sobs while doing it. "All for nothing. So many sacrifices, so much suffering. So long. All for nothing."

Opal rushes to hold her hand and whisper soothing words of comfort. To no avail. Nanny's sobs keep on trickling through the room, every single one of them an allegation to me.

I'm confused. So yes, I gave up. But I didn't hand anything to Cecilia. Certainly not my powers, because I don't have any powers. Even though I am a Gwithyas, I've never shown signs of magic abilities. Well, except when I turned my pillow into water. But that was because of the Void and things are different here. Anyone can do magic in the Void. At least I think so. Anyway, that's not important. What is important, at least I think it is, is that Nanny is wrong. Cecilia does not have the zircon. It was in Sophie's bracelet. I was holding it, and I am still holding it. I open my hand. The zircon is there all right, all small and orange and shiny. I stretch out my hand to show it to Nanny.

"I have the gem."

Nanny ignores me and continues to snivel, but my sisters do look. Their eyes widen when they see the gem in my hand. For a moment they are dumbstruck, but then their lips part into beaming grins.

"I knew it!" cheers Opal. "I knew he'd do it!"

Nanny stops her lament to see what is going on. Her eyes nearly pop out of their sockets when she spots the gem. "How . . ." she gasps

"Cecilia gave it to me," I explain. "I don't know why she did."

Nanny's hand shoots forward and grabs my wrist. "She did nothing of the sort! She placed it in you hand because she needed you to touch it so you'd hand over your control of it, and your powers, while you were weak and alone. And I saw it happen. You gave up! Cecilia defeated you."

Her bony fingers are cold on my skin. She splutters, opening and closing her mouth like a fish on dry land. It takes her a while to get her words out: "It cannot be."

"Looks like it is, though," I point out. "I'm here, and so is the zircon."

Nanny says nothing. She just sits there, her fingers hooked around my wrist, her mouth thin and pale. Opal and Amethyst shift their gazes from me to Nanny to the zircon and back. Since no one else seems inclined to speak, I ask, "So, do you reckon there's still a chance of me saving the world?"

Nanny lets go of my arm.

"No," she says, deflating back into her chair. "It is too late. You are here to die."

She gestures at a window. Of course there wasn't a window earlier, but that's how things work in the Void. It takes me two steps to reach the window which looks out into Jago and Nathaniel's room.

They are both there, looking rather glum. Joanna is there as well. She's sitting next to the fireplace with a limp body in her arms.

"That's your body," says Opal.

"You stopped breathing, and your heartbeat is fading," says Amethyst.

I observe my near-corpse. I appreciate the uniqueness of the experience—not many people get to witness their own death—but I can't say I appreciate the experience itself. The body, *my* body, isn't a pretty sight. There is blood and exposed flesh everywhere, arms and legs are bent in anatomically impossible angles with ragged bone-edges piercing even more ragged skin, and the bare, skinny chest is a black-and-purple bruised mess. I wouldn't have known it was me if Opal and Amethyst hadn't told me. I look at Joanna. She's hugging my bleeding body as if she is trying to keep the life in. She doesn't look well; her face and hair are clotted with dry blood, her brown skin has faded to a sickly near-white and she's crying as if she will never stop. Crying over me. I curl my fingers over the edge of the windowsill.

Joanna was there when the Koeg were killing me. She came to help me. She was fighting as hard as she could and shouting at me to hang on, but I didn't. Joanna battled the Koeg to save me, and I caused her to fail. My fault. Because Nanny is right about one thing: it weren't the Koeg who killed me, it was me. I gave up because I was scared, and in pain, and I didn't believe anyone cared about me anymore. I chose to die.

In the room below, Joanna buries her face in my messy hair. Her body is shaking with sobs. I press my hands onto the glass.

"What will happen to Joanna once I am dead?" I ask. "Will the doorway cease to exist? Will Joanna be stuck here forever?"

Nanny snorts. "If that was all, if the death of the Gwithyas could keep the Void locked, Angus Gwithyas would've gladly sacrificed his life. He was brave, he was a true hero. Unlike you."

Those words succeed in making me feel even worse about myself, but they don't answer my question, so I repeat, "What will happen when I die?"

"When you die," answers Nanny in a low voice, "Graham's madness will roam free. There will be nothing and nobody left to control the doorway, and the Koeg will open it, break into reality and destroy everything we hold dear."

"Really?" I ask. "But that makes no sense. If my death would free the Koeg, then what is the deal with the zircon? Why did Cecilia want it?"

"It does not matter," says Nanny dismissively. "All is lost. I thought you were the one who would end the suffering but you only made it worse. You are just as bad as Graham. I told him not to meddle with forces he couldn't understand, but he did not listen. Just like you."

Yep. There we go again: it's all stupid Zircon's fault. I'm getting so fed up with this. I leave the window and march over to Nanny.

"What do you mean I didn't listen?" I bark. "I have always listened, but no one could be bothered to tell me what the hell was going on. So I have an idea: why don't you change that right now. Explain to me in clear English what I have to do to make things right."

Nanny's eyes widen. For a moment I think I glimpse something like respect, but then she shakes her head and gestures at the window, at my broken body. "You've had your chance. You have only seconds left to live. You cannot do anything once you are dead."

"Then help me to live."

Nanny scoffs and asks, "Do I look like a necromancer?"

It occurs to me that if there were such a thing as a standard necromancer-look Nanny would nail it, but I don't say so. There wouldn't be any point anyway, because the old biddy utters a quivering sigh, shuts her eyes and starts pulling fuzzes off her dress again. I turn to my sisters.

"What about you? You two helped me before, when I was ill. Can't you do something now?"

Opal shakes her head. "All we did was help you to access your own strength. We are not healers."

"But someone else is," Amethyst says quietly.

"Who?" Opal and I ask at the same moment.

Amethyst gives Opal a funny look. "You know."

"Oh," says Opal. "Oh, yes." She glances over her shoulder at Nanny, who's still deeply engrossed in fuzz-picking, and whispers, "She won't like that."

I'm confused. Nanny is a healer?

"I know," says Amethyst. "But it's not her decision, is it? And he'd do it, I'm certain he would. He knows what's at stake."

She said 'he', so it's not Nanny.

"Who are you talking about?" I ask.

"But what if he fails?" ponders Opal.

I ask again, a little louder, "Who?"

"It's the only thing we can still try," says Amethyst.

This is becoming annoying. I wave my hands in front of my sisters' faces and ask, "What can we try? Who is a healer?"

"Jago," whispers Opal, casting another anxious glance at Nanny.

"Jago?" I whisper back, though I have no idea why we're whispering.

"He was a trained physician before he arrived here," says Opal. "There's a chance he could save your life."

I look out the window. Jago is kneeling next to Joanna, his hand on my bloody head, his back hunched and his head down. He looks like a man battered into submission, incapable of doing anything.

"I'm sure that if he could he would've done it already," I say.

"He doesn't know that he can," says Amethyst.

"But we could do for him what we did for you," adds Opal. "We can help him find his full mind power."

Mind power. Hah. A typical phrase for my out-there sisters.

It's funny. Only a few days ago, or what seems like a few days, I'd have rolled my eyes on hearing such airy-fairy gibberish. That's different now. I'm different now. I'm actually taking my sisters seriously. Seems I've become all open-minded. Not surprising considering that there's a huge gash in my head. No. Bad pun. Awful, in fact. I reign in my rambling mind and ask, "So you're saying that Jago could stop me from dying?"

"Perhaps," says Amethyst.

"Perhaps not," says Opal.

They sound as if they're announcing the loss of the last dry cracker on Earth. I squint at them. "So what aren't you telling me?"

Opal and Amethyst look at each other, and then at Nanny.

"He'd need to repair your wounds with the power of his mind," says Amethyst. "That would take a lot of energy."

"Possibly too much," adds Opal.

There's a creak from the other side of the room. Nanny has come to her warbled senses again and glowers at the girls. "I heard that," she says. "I will not let it happen. Jago will not risk his life for a nincompoop like Zircon."

Risk his life? Those words blot out the whole nincompoop comment, and I ask my sisters, "What does she mean risk his life? Could helping me kill Jago?"

Amethyst shuffles her feet, just like she used to do back home. "Perhaps."

"Perhaps not," says Opal, casting another skittish look at Nanny, who reacts with a piercing glare back and snarls, "I said no!"

I find myself agreeing with her. "I can't let a man die for me," I tell Opal and Amethyst. "Well, it depends on the man, obviously. I wouldn't mind sacrificing some murderous dictator, but not Jago."

"For once the brat speaks sense," says Nanny. "Listen to him." She points a bony finger at my sisters and they both shudder at the sight. I wonder what experiences they have with Nanny's pointing.

Opal composes herself and says, "Think about it, Zircon. Jago is a good man, yes, but he's not the Gwithyas, and he cannot stop the Koeg."

"Plus, he wouldn't think twice about it," says Amethyst.

"I said no!" screeches Nanny, and Opal and Amethyst leap back, just in time to escape the projectile that Nanny has fired at them, which lands on the floor with a light pop. It's a nail. A gnarled, yellow nail with strings of red tissue trailing off it. I look at Nanny. Her finger is still pointing, but the tip is ragged and covered in blood.

"She does that when she's angry," says Amethyst, kicking aside the bloody nail.

Right. It wouldn't be my choice of persuasion, but I still agree with Nanny's sentiments.

"If Nanny is so opposed to it, she probably has a good reason," I say.

"Her judgement is blurred by personal issues," says Amethyst.

"Like what?" I ask, and then I shrug. "It doesn't matter. I won't let Jago risk his life for me."

"Understandable," says Opal. "But irrelevant. Sorry Zircon, but there's more at stake here than you and your sensitivities, more than Nanny's feelings, and even, however sad, more than Jago's life. Besides, Amethyst is right. Jago wouldn't think twice about making this sacrifice."

She takes Amethyst's hand, and then they are gone. Or no, not gone. They've become orange lights again, and they float over my chest. My real, crushed chest, down in the Void room. Opal and Amethyst, in their orange soul form, blink and bounce in front of Joanna, Jago and Nathaniel. Joanna and Nathaniel don't budge, it's obvious they see nothing, but Jago jerks up, stares at the lights for a few moments, and then reaches for them.

"What is it?" asks Nathaniel, but Jago says nothing. He tilts his head to the left, as if he's listening, which he probably is, because he slowly nods and then places both hands on my chest.

Behind me, Nanny growls, "They did it, the pesky little trollops. Well, then. If my son is going for it, you should at least give it a try."

My mouth falls open. Her *son*? Down in the Void room Jago's eyes roll back in their sockets and he howls as if he's being torn to pieces as his strong fingers dig into my bruised, shredded skin. A surge of power rams into my body, and the pain is back.

CHAPTER 14
Alive

IT BURNS. IN MY THROAT FIRST, AND THEN IN MY CHEST, AND IN my entire body. Every time I take in air, it burns as if I'm inside a pottery oven. That seems unfair. I'm only breathing. Someone is rocking me. Opal? Amethyst? Then she speaks, and her voice washes over me like a warm shower. Joanna. She is snivelling in my neck. Her breath warms my ear as she whispers into it, "Stay with me, sweetie. Please. It'll be okay, I'm here. I'm with you."

Sweetie? Wow. And she's stroking my face. She even gives me little kisses on my forehead, and on my hair. I must be hallucinating. A sharp pain tears through my chest, agonising enough to stunt my breathing. That's definitely not a hallucination. I struggle to get my respiratory system going again, and am rather proud when I succeed. I lick my lips, which feels as if I am rubbing a chunk of wood over pieces of cardboard, and croak, "It hurts."

Joanna goes rigid. "What?" she asks, but I can't form another coherent phrase, not just yet, so I just groan.

"He's waking up!" gasps Joanna.

There's another voice and I hear the shuffling of feet, but I can't see anything. Someone touches my chest. "His heart is beating stronger," says a man. "That's bloody impossible."

"He needs something to drink," says Joanna. "Give me a cup of that stuff."

"This is wrong," the man says. "He was dying."

"Nathaniel!" snaps Joanna. "Give me that cup!"

"But . . ."

"Now!" growls Joanna, and he must've obeyed her, because moments later she puts a cup to my lips and says, "Drink this. It'll help against the pain."

I drink with small sips. It's the smoked cinnamon concoction again. It makes me all warm inside, and Joanna was right, it numbs the pain. Good stuff this. I wonder if it's morphine. Of course it isn't. I'm in the Void. No anaesthetics here. I'm so light now. So light, and I float away.

In my dreams I have no need for glasses, for my eyes are sharp as those of a peregrine falcon. Cecilia is dressed in rags and looks like a child caught in a famine: protruding ribs, bloated belly, patchy hair and sunken eyes.

"You messed everything up!" she moans. "You horrible boy. We should've killed you when we had the chance, before you became the Guardian."

She's sitting cross-legged on the floor and eyes me with obvious dismay. "You should've let me have the zircon. I tried so hard to get my hands on that gem," she sulks.

"You did," I agree. "I don't understand why though. You don't actually need the gem to get into my world, do you? My death would be sufficient. What did you want with the zircon?"

Cecilia rolls her eyes until they are backwards in their sockets. Somehow the bloody backsides of her eyeballs still manage to express contempt.

"You are so stupid. Yes, once you're dead the Koeg would be free and able to enter your world. But then what? They would simply destroy everything until there was another Void. Boooring. I don't want the Koeg to be free. Did you know I too have magic? Not as much as Graham, but more than Jago, and certainly more than my stupid brother. And I have learned so much in here: to create Koeg, to kill humans, and I even learned to compose and cast spells. I learned that from you, and from all your ancestors. Did you know that, Gwithyas? It was always me hiding inside that old witch when you performed the ritual. You and your predecessors banished me again and again, but I always returned to watch and learn. And now all I need is the focus, the last gem, so I can add your powers to mine and open the Void, and then I will be the greatest sorceress who ever existed. I will rule the world."

I blink. Cecilia in the role of omnipotent overlord hadn't occurred to me yet. I guess I shouldn't be surprised. She's not the sort who cares about anyone's well-being, and that includes the Koeg. I almost feel sorry for the twisted critters. All they ever got was a dull half-life in a grotty semi-void, and all they have to look forward to is becoming the puppets of an insane 18th-century pre-teen.

"Do you like my plan?" enquires Cecilia.

"No," I say. "And I have no intention of letting you execute it."

She grins, exposing a set of green tooth stumps. "Let's talk about something else." She points at a quivering blob behind her. "Look, one of us got a taste of your precious world already. You couldn't prevent that, could you?"

The blob crawls towards me, oozing blood and rotting flesh. I can't tell which end is front or back as there is no difference; both sport outsized jaws with triple rows of teeth. I don't recall ever seeing this particular Koeg before. It's holding something in one of its mouths and it shakes it, spraying decaying tissue over my trousers. I gag and back away.

"Aw," says Cecilia. "You hurt his feelings." She pats the atrocity on what I assume is its back. "You don't remember him, do you? Shame on you, he's a close relative. Grown on your shoulder, from your uncle's flesh."

I do remember. Without wanting it, I place my hand on my

throat. Cecilia smiles widely, which causes her lips to burst. While droplets of blood and pus dribble over her chin as she says, "You are so easily distracted by physical discomfort, Gwithyas. When my little friend here was choking you, you faltered, and the doorway opened just far enough for him to leap through to your world. Only when your girlfriend started slashing at us was he dragged back in. Still, he had enough time in your world to bring us a souvenir. Wanna see?" She clicks her knuckle bones. "Give," she says, and the toothy Koeg drops its toy in her hand. Cecilia carefully unfolds it, and while she is doing this she speaks to me. She sound tired and old but determined when she says, "We know you now, Gwithyas. We've pierced your mind, we know how to break you. We almost had you, and we shall not fail again. Your girlfriend won't be able to rescue you the next time and you still don't know how to stop us, do you? Talking about your girlfriend, she's kissing mister Goldilocks as we speak. What do you think of that?" She pouts her lips to make small smacking noises that gradually get louder and louder until they ram into my ears and my head and turn into words: *'Joanna and Nathaniel sitting in a tree, K – I – S – S – I – N – GEE!'*"

Joanna and Nathaniel. Nathaniel and Joanna. Is she lying?

"Oh no," sniggers Cecilia. "It is the truth. You didn't really think she'd ever love *you*, did you?" She points at me with a wriggly bony finger. "Ah, the disillusionments you suffer. But an unfaithful shield isn't the worst of your problems, Gwithyas. We are. The Koeg are recuperating and next time you won't stand a chance."

She has unfolded the toothy Koeg's souvenir and holds it up for me to see. "It took my friend only a few seconds to get this, Gwithyas. Look at it, and see what we are capable of."

She holds up a face, neatly scraped off its skull. It has sleek black hair and is wearing really thick glasses. It's Ms Chen, the optometrist. I wake up to the sound of my own screams.

"It's okay, Zircon, you're safe."

I open my eyes and see the fluffy blur that I've come to recognise as Joanna. She's stroking my hair. I hope it isn't too greasy. It tends to get greasy if I don't wash it every day. I try to focus, to see Joanna more clearly, but my useless eyes don't cooperate. I can just make out the shape of her eyes: still almonds.

"Zircon? Can you hear me?"

Of course I can. But I suppose she wants a spoken confirmation. That isn't easy. I huff, I puff, and eventually manage to utter, "Yeah."

I sound like an asthmatic kitten. Joanna mumbles something that sounds suspiciously religious and asks, "How are you feeling?"

I ponder on that and try to sense my body. It is not an uplifting experience. My chest still burns and throbs with every breath, and when I try to move it's as if my skeleton is slicing its way through my muscles. But explaining all that would be too much of an effort, so I say, "Sore."

A flurry of golden locks appears in my limited field of vision. Nathaniel.

"Only sore?" He leans over me until his shiny hair is all I can see. His voice is hoarse and his words clipped. "You are recovering fast. Too fast. We need to talk, Zircon."

"Not now, Nathaniel," says Joanna. "He almost died, remember?"

"Yes," replies Nathaniel. "And it's the *almost* that bothers me." He prods at my aching chest. "Why didn't the Koeg kill you?"

"Stop that, Nathaniel!" snarls Joanna. There's a slapping sound and the chest-prodding stops abruptly.

"Ouch," mumbles Nathaniel.

Joanna doesn't sound at all compassionate when she hisses at him, "What the hell is wrong with you?"

"What is wrong with *you*?" retorts Nathaniel. "You saw what he did to Jago."

Jago! I remember now. He healed me, like Opal and Amethyst said he would. I need to know what happened to him. I need to know if he died. I try to ask, but before I can utter as much as a single word Joanna says, "And *you* heard what Jago said. Zircon didn't do it."

Jago said something? I hope that means that he's not dead, but I keep in mind that Opal and Amethyst are also rather chatty for dead people.

"Even so, Zircon needs to tell us about the Koeg," insists Nathaniel. "And he needs to do it now."

"Why?" asks Joanna. "There were no Koeg when we went out to hunt earlier, were there?"

Out? Joanna and Nathaniel went out, together? I suddenly feel a lot sicker and utter a miserable groan. Joanna reacts instantly. "What is it, Zircon? Are you okay?"

Of course I'm not okay. I feel like a squashed earwig. Or what I imagine a squashed earwig would feel like. I probably look it too, and Joanna has been hunting Koeg alongside handsome brave Nathaniel who has nothing earwiggish about him. I can picture them courageously fighting off ghastly monsters, Nathaniel's muscles bulging while he smashes yet another foul entity to bits, Joanna sneaking admiring glances at him. Gross. And here's me getting my hopes up because she is so sweet to me. What was I thinking? I'm so weak and pathetic that she feels sorry for me, that's all it is. I shouldn't delude myself. There's no way she'd fancy a visually impaired ginger geek if she can have Nathaniel. They belong together. No one belongs with me. I have no sisters, no parents, and no girlfriend. I wish I had stayed dead. I don't realise that I'm crying until Joanna brushes the tears from my face.

"You have to listen to me, Joanna," insists Nathaniel. "He needs to explain."

"Leave him alone," says Joanna. "Just leave him alone."

I must've fallen asleep. And it must've been a long nap, because when I wake up Joanna has grown a beard.

"Hello Gwithyas," she says in a peculiarly deep voice. It's not Joanna but Jago. This is my chance to check on his vivacity status.

"Are you dead?" I ask.

"No," Jago says hesitantly. "I'm fairly certain that I am not."

"You saved me," I say. "They said you would. But they said you might die. I didn't want you to do it. I'm sorry. I'm glad you're okay. You are okay, aren't you?"

Jago puts his hand on my forehead. "Hush," he says. "Don't get yourself so worked up. You need to rest."

I think he's avoiding my question, so I ask again, "Are you okay?"

"As well as can be expected," says Jago. A politician's answer. Meaningless and intended to distract. He's avoiding my question all right. Which means he's not okay. At least he's alive, I guess I ought to be grateful for that.

"Who told you that I'd heal you?" Jago asks.

"Opal and Amethyst," I say, and it occurs to me that those aren't their real names, and that I never even asked for their real names. I'm such a jerk. I quickly change the topic.

"Your mum didn't want you to heal me. She didn't want you to risk your life."

Jago's fingers on my forehead tense up. "The witch?"

"Yes. I didn't know she was your mother. I should've known, of course, because I knew that she was Angus's wife, and you did say that he's your father. I'm sorry. I mean, not sorry that she's your mum, but sorry that she's in the Void too, like you. You must've missed her when you were little."

"I didn't," Jago says in a clipped manner. He takes his hand off my head. "She was still there, remember? In the tower. I used to see her every month."

"Oh, yes," I say, and I imagine this horrible scene of a little boy in the tower room, trying to speak to his possessed mother who is chained up in a rocking chair. Now that makes for one massive childhood trauma. Did she lash that purple tongue at her own son too? Did she shoot her fingernails at him? A chill runs over my back. Clearly this isn't a great topic of conversation either, so I change the subject again and ask where Joanna is. I want to know that anyway.

"She's on patrol," says Jago. "She and Nathaniel are checking the area for Koeg activity."

Again? I grimace.

"They found nothing," Jago says reassuringly, misinterpreting my tortured expression. "Not a single Koeg."

"Yeah. Great," I grumble.

"It is unprecedented," continues Jago. "I don't know how you did it, but you have completely silenced the Koeg. There is no trace of them. I've never been this at ease since I entered the Void. Thank you. I'm sorry that you were so badly injured in the process."

"Oh, but I'm feeling okay now," I say, and it's true. I'm tired, sure, and stiff, but there's no pain.

"You do not need to put on a brave face," Jago says.

Brave? Me? He obviously doesn't know me very well.

"I'm fine, really," I say. "Thanks to you."

"I see," says Jago. "In that case, could I have a look at your wounds?"

I say that it's fine, and Jago starts unwrapping my heavily bandaged left arm. I brace myself for the pain, but it doesn't come. Once the bandages are off Jago says, "The wounds have closed. That is remarkable. Wait."

He pulls, unwraps and cuts bandages off numerous parts of my body and gathers them next to me. When he is done, I touch the heap of fabric. It's the size of a solid sofa cushion. I must've looked like an Egyptian mummy.

Jago whistles between his teeth. "Nathaniel was right. You are recovering fast."

"I told you I'm good," I say.

"Good enough to eat?" Jago doesn't wait for a reply, but moves about and then holds a bowl under my nose. "You should eat. You haven't had anything solid since you were injured."

The food—I suppose it's squashed Koeg again—smells mouth-watering. My stomach rumbles. "I'm starving," I say.

Jago helps me to sit, props some cushions in my back and hands me the bowl and a spoon. Forgetting anything that resembles table manners, I scoff the lumpy blurb as fast as I can swallow it. Who'd have thought that squashed Koeg could taste this delicious? I even lick the last slimy bits out of the bowl.

"I think I can safely state that you are well on your way to making a full recovery," says Jago.

I've just finished my third bowl of Koeg puree when Joanna and Nathaniel return.

"No Koeg," reports Joanna, and then she gasps, "Zircon! You're up!"

She rushes over and kneels down next to me, touching my hands and my face. Her hands are soft and warm, and I can't hold back a probably rather smug grin.

"Yeah," I say. "I'm fine, actually."

Joanna touches the scars on my arm. "Thank God."

Nathaniel appears behind her, a tall blur with a golden halo. "God had nothing to do with this," he says.

I think he wants to say more, and I have a feeling that it's nothing particularly kind, but all he does is huff contemptuously and pace away. Joanna hasn't reacted to him at all. She's too engrossed in stroking me. I'm not sure how to take that. It's nice that Joanna is suddenly being so affectionate and all, and since it's what I wanted ever since I knew she existed, I ought to be thrilled. And I am, of course I am, but I'm also feeling really awkward, so I just sit rigidly between my pillows and fiddle with the empty bowl in my hand. To make matters worse Joanna is shaking. I think she's crying. That's not cool. I'm not good with weepy women. Or weepy men, for that matter. Weeping just isn't my thing. I try to divert her attention.

"We need to get out of here," I say. "We need a plan."

It works. Joanna snorts noisily and asks, "Do you have one?"

"Have one what?"

"A plan."

"No," I admit.

"Never mind," says Joanna. "We'll find a way out. Now that the Koeg are gone there's no hurry. We are not in danger."

"They're not gone," I say. "They can't be gone, because they can't die."

Joanna gently squeezes my arm. "Of course they're gone," she says soothingly, as if I'm a scared little boy who requires reassuring. "Nat and I have looked everywhere. There is nothing left of the Koeg."

So it's Nat now. Yeah, I guess the level of intimacy between them would increase after spending so much time together. I shouldn't be surprised. And I'm not, but it certainly peeves me off. I pull my arm away from Joanna's reassuring hand and snap, "Well, I guess you and *Nat* must've missed something, because I just spoke to Cecilia. The Koeg are still here, and they are regrouping as we speak."

"Regrouping?" asks Joanna.

"Nat?" asks Jago, but I don't think he's talking to me.

"Cecilia?" asks Nathaniel. *He* is definitely talking to me, and I don't like his tone. It's as if he is accusing me of something.

"Yes, Cecilia," I reply. "I'm sure you've met her. She's some sort of girly uber-Koeg. Anyway, she said that the Koeg are getting ready, and next time they will succeed. They will go through the door and destroy the world. We need to stop them."

"And how do we do that?" asks Joanna.

"I don't know. But I know someone who does. Graham Gwithyas."

"Ah," says Jago.

Joanna pats my hand. "Sweetie, Graham Gwithyas has been dead a very long time."

She called me sweetie again. Pity that she said it in the way you'd talk to an intoxicated lunatic.

"He's not dead," I say. "Not completely anyway. I met him when I was dead. And he . . ."

Jago interrupts me. "Perhaps you are not yet as well as I thought. You need to rest."

"No," I object. "I need the zircon."

"He's confused," whispers Joanna, apparently under the impression that I can't hear her even though she's sitting right next to me. "He doesn't even know who he is anymore. He's looking for himself."

"Not Zircon!" I say. "I don't need me. I mean, of course I do, but I meant that I need the stone. The gem."

"Oh, that zircon," says Joanna.

"Yes. That zircon."

"You did seem awfully attached to it," says Joanna. "You were still hanging on to it when you were unconscious. Here it is."

She drops the zircon in my hand. It is cold and solid on my skin. I mutter thanks and fold my fingers around it. It feels just like any stone. How can this possibly be so significant? And more importantly, how do I use it? I move the zircon to my other hand and wait. Nothing happens. I close my eyes. Still nothing. Except that I suddenly feel really really tired. Someone grabs my upper arms and gently helps me lie down.

"You need to rest."

Yeah, I guess I do. With the zircon in my hand I doze off.

I am back in the kitchen. I know it the moment that I feel the freezing slate floor through my boxers. I leap up, clutching the zircon, ready to slap away aggressive Koeg, but there are none. The kitchen is empty except for a burly figure with tousled ginger hair who is kneeling in front of the fireplace. I say his name.

"Graham?"

He turns around. His eyes are bloodshot, his eyelids swollen. "Who are you?"

"My name is Zircon," I introduce myself, and I open my hand. "Like this stone. It was from your wife's bracelet, wasn't it?"

He reaches out to touch the gem, but I close my fist and pull my arm back. Graham doesn't insist. He continues to look at my fist and whispers, "That is what remains of her. A small gemstone and," He points at the fireplace, at the pile of skulls in there, "one of those. I don't even know which one."

I decide to not point out to him that it's entirely his fault that Sophie is now a skull in a fireplace.

"Who are you?" repeats Graham. "Or *what* are you? I saw you when Sophie died, and then . . ." He doesn't finish his sentence, just gives me a puzzled look.

"I am your descendant, the last Gwithyas," I say, and I point at my hair. "Can't you see the resemblance? Apparently we are very much alike, you and I. But there is one important difference."

Graham rises from his kneeling position. That unsettles me. He is at least a head taller than I am and has a significantly more impressive physique. He must've seemed a giant in his time. He slaps some dust from his trousers, dust that might well be Sophie's decomposed skin; another thing I better not mention.

"How are you different from me?" he asks.

"You created the Void," I say. "And I will destroy it."

I'm quite pleased with this valiant one-liner, but I take a step back just in case Graham objects to my plan. He doesn't. He nods. "It has to end. Do as you wish. I shall not hinder you."

I can't believe what I'm hearing. Graham Gwithyas, the mad and mighty warlock, doesn't want to kill me. I better take advantage of this unexpected good fortune.

"I need your help," I say. "Ehm, the thing is, I don't actually how to destroy the Void. Plus, those Koeg have become pretty strong over time. I need your magic to stop them."

Graham produces a joyless, derisive snigger. "My magic? My magic was useless. I could not stop them. You saw it. You witnessed my disgrace. I could not control the Koeg. I could not control my own mind."

"Yeah," I admit, "you did mess up a little there. A lot actually.

But still, you know how to use the power of the hill, and I don't. You could show me how to do it."

"You do not know?"

"No," I say. "I was never told."

"But then how . . ." Graham shakes his head. "But you are here. You are speaking to me. That alone requires an ability to control a magic force greater than I have ever achieved."

"Yeah well," I say, "that may be so, but it sure isn't me who is doing the magic. I only fell asleep. But I am the last Gwithyas, so I seriously need to stop the Koeg. Tell me how. All I know is that I need to use this somehow."

I wave the gem about. Graham follows its movement with his eyes. "The gem. Yes. Merryn used the gem."

Now who the Void is Merryn?

"She was my son's wife," Graham conveniently explains. "She was also a powerful witch. I disliked her. She disliked me even more."

He takes two long steps, stops within an inch of my nose and grabs my head in his shovels of hands. I squirm, but Graham doesn't let go. He shakes my head so his blood-stained shirt becomes a grubby blur to my eyes.

"It is here!" he growls. "All in here. The demons, the rage, the void. My insanity. This is why every single Gwithyas ends their life raving mad. This is what the witch has done to our family."

Suddenly he lets go of my head. I scurry back as fast as I can until I stand with my back against the wall. Graham brushes his hand over his forehead. "I had no control," he mutters, "no boundaries, no form. Only madness." His arm shoots forward and he points at my hand with the gem in it. "Control! That is what the gem is for. Smooth, hard, unbending. Part of the magic of the Earth." He takes a deep breath. "You say you do not know. You say you need my help. Very well. I shall do what I can. Give me your hand, the one with the gem in it."

I hesitate.

"You don't trust me," says Graham. "That is understandable."

He says nothing else. No attempts to convince me or to redeem himself. He just stands there, large and ginger, with his hand outstretched, and he allows me to think it over.

So here I am, with Graham Gwithyas, the greatest and maddest warlock of all times. Thanks to him my parents are bog bodies, the optician is faceless, I'm losing my mind and the world is about to end. Yet right now, the way he stands there, Graham sort of reminds me of my father: a little out if it, sure, but predominantly tired and sad. And I trust him. I place my hand in his so we are both holding the zircon.

"The last gem," he says. "I gave Sophie one for every five years we had been together. I loved her more than anything. To confine my wayward mind Merryn needed something that held meaning to me. She used the gems that represented my love for my wife, and that is how she managed to bind my lunacy."

His fingers close so hard around mine that it hurts. Perhaps I shouldn't have trusted him after all. I try to pull myself free, but Graham is far stronger than I am. He continues to clasp my hand and shuts his eyes.

"Let our memories merge," he mumbles. "Let us share our thoughts."

The whole thing reminds me of a Vulcan mind-meld in an episode of Star Trek, with Graham as Mr. Spock and me as a pathetic copy of Kirk. Not that I'm getting anything out of it, but it seems as if Graham does. At first, his face is stern. Then he starts to laugh. A loud, booming laugh. Not quite the muahaha of your average mad evil guy, but close.

"The flames," he guffaws. "You extinguished the flames!" His eyes flash open and bore into mine. "Gwithyas," he whispers, "if anyone has ever been worthy, it is you. You do not need me. I surrender to you, Gwithyas. Take it all. Take my demons, take my Void, take my insanity!"

He laughs again as an avalanche of unfamiliar memories, images, thoughts and most of all, delusions, cascades into my consciousness. I can't make head or tails of it, and it just keeps coming.

"It's too fast!" I shout. "It's too much. Let me go!"

Graham lets go of my hand and steps back. He grins bare a set of tobacco-stained teeth and raises his hands.

"Control the Void!" he thunders. "Control the Koeg."

CHAPTER 15
Warlock

"ZIRCON!"

That's not Graham. I force my eyes open and distinguish a halo of golden locks. Nathaniel.

"Uggah?" I ask, or something along those lines.

"Are you awake?"

I rub my eyes. "Yeah, obviously. No chance of sleeping with you shouting in my ear like that."

"Good," whispers Nathaniel. "Because the others are in the kitchen and you and I need to have a little private conversation."

Somehow that sounds wrong. Nathaniel moves his face so close to mine that I can smell his breath when he speaks. It smells of cinnamon.

"It's peculiar, Zircon. You healing so quickly. And the Koeg seem to be attracted to you. I wonder why that is."

There is something about his tone of voice that puts me on yellow alert.

"They just attack anyone," I say. "Because they're evil."

The golden locks sway from left to right. "No," says Nathaniel. "There's more to it than that. They have never shown that much interest in Jago or me. They targeted you specifically, and they could've killed you but they didn't. Now why did they let you live?"

I open my mouth to answer him, but he doesn't wait for my reply. He is more interested in putting across his own thoughts.

"You used Jago to recover from your injuries. You would've killed him too, if I hadn't intervened."

"Intervened?"

"Yes. I pulled him off you before you could drain all his energy. Because you didn't care about that, did you? You wanted him dead, didn't you?"

"What?" I ask. "Are you nuts? Why would I want to kill Jago?"

"You tell me," says Nathaniel. "You're the one who spoke to Cecilia, and who wanted to speak to Graham. That's a little suspicious, isn't it?"

"Not really?" I squeak hopefully.

"No? You do not think it's a little suspicious? Because I do."

Nathaniel sounds positively threatening now. I better come up with a convincing response.

"N-no," I stammer. "I don't want to talk to Cecilia but she just keeps bugging me and I only wanted to talk to Graham so I can learn how to control the Koeg."

"I knew it!"

A sharp, hard object presses against the skin of my neck. I think it's a dagger. The yellow alert rapidly turns to a hysterical red.

"So I was right," barks Nathaniel. "You're one of them. You are an ally of the Koeg, just like my sister. That's why you're still alive!"

His sister? What in the Void is he on about? Then I remember the badly spelled letter. And Nathaniel's name on the family tree. His name, and Cecilia's, close together. Oh great. Another traumatised ancestor. Cursed be those family ties.

"I didn't know you were Cecilia's brother," I say, but my words are drowned by rapid footsteps and Joanna's shouting, "No, Nathaniel! Let him go!

"Leave me to it," growls Nathaniel. "Don't even think of

stopping me or I will stab him to his miserable death. I know what I'm doing."

I seriously doubt that he does, but I am not in a position to argue. The dagger is pressing harder into my neck. I think it's drawing blood. Nathaniel's hand is shaking; one false move could turn my artery into a gruesome imitation of a geyser.

"You are one of them," cries Nathaniel. "You betrayed us all. You even betrayed your own family. Your own father and mother!"

At the mention of my parents my feelings of panic come to a full stop. As I remember their drained bodies on flowery sheets, I forget everything else, even the knife on my throat. Eyeballs dangling from the ceiling. No no no, it was not my fault. I didn't betray them. My head gets hot. *I did not!*

"Shut up!" I roar, and I push Nathaniel away. He rockets backwards and crashes into a pile of chests. I jump up and soar over to him. My head is burning, but I don't care. I grab Nathaniel by the collar of his shirt and lift him. He weighs less than a wireless mouse. I ram his squirming body against the wall.

"Do not dare speak of my parents," I bellow. "And don't you even *suggest* that I'd work with the Koeg. I am here to destroy them, to destroy the Void. I shall take revenge more ferociously than even they can imagine. I shall turn their essence to ashes. They killed Sophie. They killed my sisters. They killed Mum. They killed Dad. They are dead, all of them. Dead. Like . . . like . . ."

The haunting image of my dead parents in their bed returns with a vengeance. Suddenly Nathaniel has his weight back again and I have to let him go.

'D-dead," I stammer while Nathaniel drops on the floor like a bag of damp laundry. He doesn't stay down for long. While I am standing watery-eyed in front of the scattered boxes, he leaps to his feet and waves his dagger at my throat.

"Nathaniel! Stop!"

Jago's baritone is calm and composed as always. "Leave

him alone. Don't you see? He's not like your sister. He is the Guardian."

I'm sitting cross-legged on the floor with my elbows on my knees and my face hidden behind my hands. I can't bring myself to look up or to speak or to move. I fear that if I do any of those things, I will shatter into a million pieces. I said it. Mum, Dad, Opal and Amethyst are dead. I'm the only one left. I'm alone. It's peculiar: all that time I've known this, but somehow it wasn't real, not until I said it out loud.

Joanna sits next to me. I hear her breathe and I smell her, too. A sweet mixture of smoke and jasmine. I wonder how she got that jasmine. Perhaps it is in her shampoo or deodorant or something. Pretty persistent stuff if I can still discern it after so long in the Void. The smoke-scent must be from the fire.

Joanna softly says my name. "Zircon?" She tugs at my hands. "Zircon, put your hands down. Look at me."

I'm so numb that it doesn't even occur to me to disobey. Joanna's face is a misty brown blot. "I'm sorry," says the blot. "I'm so sorry."

"What for?"

I don't recognise the voice that asks this, so quiet and hoarse, but since it comes from my mouth it must be mine.

"I'm sorry about your parents, and your sisters."

"Oh."

"I didn't know. If I had known I would have . . ."

"It doesn't matter," I interrupt her. "They've been dead quite a while now. Especially my sisters. They aren't even my sisters. They were already dead when you spoke to them, did you know that? You have chatted to their souls. I never really had any sisters. I did have parents though. When we went through the gate their corpses were lying right next to us. But their eyes are here. You saw them dangle from the ceiling in the blood room. Remember?"

Joanna doesn't reply so I keep talking. I barely know what

I'm saying, the words tumble from my mouth. "I'm an orphan now, just like you. Two lost orphans, trapped in the Void. Not that it matters. What is there to go back for? There's no one left who cares about me. Oh, but you have your uncle. I have an uncle too, but he tried to kill me. He does tricks, my uncle. He can pull his stomach out through his mouth."

Joanna's places her hands on my cheeks. "You're rambling, Zircon. Pull yourself together. Breathe in."

I do as she says.

"And now out, and then take a really deep breath in."

Again, I follow the orders like a well-trained puppy. It helps. My thoughts become less disorganised. Joanna's grip on my face loosens. Her fingers run softly over my temples. "Better?"

"A little," I say, not wanting her to stop stroking me. I shouldn't have worried. Her hands move down over my neck and behind my shoulders. Her face comes closer, and then her lips touch mine.

When Joanna pulls away again I touch my lips. Surely they must've changed. Something as life-altering as my first proper kiss simply cannot have happened without leaving some sort of mark.

"You never did this before, did you?" asks Joanna.

No, I hadn't. But I'd hoped that wouldn't be too obvious. I've always dreaded my first kiss, thinking I wouldn't know what to do, and sure enough, I didn't. The whole thing would've been a saliva-riddled disaster if Joanna hadn't been so obviously very skilled at the matter. I reckon this wasn't exactly her first kiss. Or even her second. Which is a bit disturbing, but I guess that's how things are if you grow up in the real world instead of in a secluded manor. And she's older than I am anyway.

She's sitting a couple of feet in front of me, a dark shadow against lighter ones. I wish I could see her properly. See if she looks different now that she has kissed me. She's quiet. Perhaps she was so disgusted with my kissing that she doesn't know what to say. Perhaps she's figuring out how to tell me that without hurting my feelings. Should I talk about it? Ask her if she enjoyed it?

"You're a pretty good kisser for a beginner," says Joanna.

"Oh."

Lame response, but I can't think of anything else to say. I'm not even sure if I'm supposed to be flattered or not. *Pretty good*, she said, but also *for a beginner*. Which could mean 'rubbish but with hope of improvement'. I suppose it's better than a screech of utter revolt.

"Don't overthink this, Zircon," says Joanna. "It was good. I'd like to do it again as soon as we are out of here."

She falls silent again, and I suppose she's giving me some sort of special look, but I can't tell.

Suddenly it strikes me that I have been so absorbed with this kissing stuff that for several minutes, or what passes for minutes in the Void, I didn't spare a single thought for my butchered family. It seems that love indeed conquers everything, even debilitating grief. Or did I forget about them because I have now shared my pain? Like a sort of talking therapy? Still, it's not on. Just as a grinding sense of guilt is readying itself to settle in my consciousness, I'm startled by a loud creak. The kitchen door is opening, and there are footsteps. I recognise the sound of Jago's heavy gait, but Nathaniel is moving slowly and quietly, his feet dragging sloppily over the floor.

"Everything all right?" asks Joanna.

"More or less," says Jago. "And here?"

"We're good."

Nathaniel clears his throat. "I'm sorry."

My neck stings where he scratched me with his dagger, but I'm not in a mood to hold grudges. My lips still sizzle from Joanna's kiss, and I feel sorry for Nathaniel. Having Cecilia for a sister would make anyone edgy.

"It's fine," I say with a generous hand gesture. "We all make mistakes. No hard feelings. And I'm sorry for, ehm, for throwing you and stuff."

"I deserved no less," says Nathaniel, and he sits down. Judging by the prolonged shuffling I hear, Jago is doing the same. My presumption is confirmed when Jago's deep voice thuds straight into my left ear, "You are the Guardian. Why did you not tell us that?"

"I didn't know," I reply, rubbing my ear. "I mean, I did, but I didn't believe it. And I couldn't do magic either. I'm not even sure I can do it now. I'm not as talented as you are, Jago."

"I suspect you are a lot more talented," says Jago. "What you did to Nathaniel far exceeds my abilities."

I scoff. "Like your ability to bring an almost dead person back to life?"

"You could do the same if you'd been medically trained. And I suspect you wouldn't die from it, either."

"You didn't die."

"Only thanks to Nathaniel. He pulled me off you before my heart stopped." Jago pats my arm. "You are strong, Gwithyas. And that is fortunate, for if what you said earlier is true, and the Koeg are regrouping, your powers shall be sorely needed."

"He's right," agrees Joanna. "Come on, Zircon, whizz up an indestructible battle-axe or something."

I'm about to say that I really can't, but then I remember the fire. I did it that time. I conjured up some water and snuffed the flame-Koeg. Graham mentioned that. He seemed to think it was funny, but I also got the notion that he was impressed. It wasn't even that hard. The Void was all too willing to shape itself to my wishes. And this time it should be even easier because I have the zircon, and Graham said he'd surrender to me, whatever that meant. I should give it a try.

I turn the zircon in my hand. It gets warm. I sense the hopeful eyes of Joanna, Jago and Nathaniel on me. I wish I could see their faces. Especially Joanna's. If I'm such a great wizard you'd think that I'd be able to fix my own vision. Perhaps I can.

I concentrate and imagine that I have excellent eyesight. The air in front of me sizzles. Something falls in my lap. I pick it up.

A pair of glasses. Not exactly what I was hoping for, but I put them on anyway. The misty blur from the last few days turns into a sharp-edged tableau-vivant of white walls, boxes and three still individuals.

To my left sits Nathaniel, who for a change looks like a wrung-out mop. He is cuddled up to Jago, who is pale and looks a little withered. His beard is messy and his eyes are bloodshot. Is that the result of healing me? He stares at me and seems to be barely aware that he's rubbing Nathaniel's arm, which strikes me as a little odd. More like something a married couple would do rather than two friends who are also distant relatives. In front of me kneels Joanna. Her long lashes sweep seductively over her shining almond eyes.

"So," she says. "Are we gonna kick the Koeg's butts with your specs?"

Chapter 16
Invasion

Joanna may not be overwhelmed by my optometric magic, but Jago is positively chuffed. He can't keep his eyes off my new glasses.

"This is most impressive," he keeps muttering. "There may yet be hope."

"It's not that great," says Joanna. "You're a much better wizard, Jago. You made all the stuff in here, but that still didn't get you out of this cesspit, did it? I can't see how Zircon's glasses are so much better."

"But they are," says Jago. "Observe the detail. And the material! Have you not noted that everything I create consists of the same smooth material? That is because it is not fully formed. I lack the ability to create things that are totally real. I do not have sufficient control of the magic. Yet Zircon's glasses are truly glass. And the rim! A magnificent substance that I do not even recognise."

"Plastic," say Joanna and I at the same time, and I add, "It's an artificial material, greatly overused in our time."

"It's everywhere," says Joanna. "We have plastic bags, toys, furniture, crockery, window frames, you name it. If we get out of here you can see it for yourself."

"*When* we get out of here," Jago corrects her. "I have no

doubts that Zircon can control the Koeg. We ought to be back in reality soon."

"Soon," mumbles Nathaniel, who has so far been uncharacteristically quiet. He gives me a watery smile that looks more like a nervous tic. "I too am certain that you will lead us out of here and destroy the Void," he says, and then he gives Jago a glum look, grabs his hand and keeps hold of it. They intertwine their fingers and sit quietly, looking rather miserable. Weird. You'd think they'd be happy about leaving. Perhaps they're not as sure about my powers as they pretend to be.

"Something wrong?" I ask. A ridiculous question. We're in the Void, where pretty much everything is wrong, but Jago gets what I mean.

"Every place has some pleasant aspects," he says. "Even this one. We're merely reminiscing on those things we will miss."

I blink in surprise. "Miss? What could you possibly miss about the Void?"

"It doesn't matter," says Nathaniel dismissively.

"Is this about Cecilia?" I ask.

"No," Nathaniel says.

"You know," Joanna says so suddenly that she makes me jump. "Plastic isn't the only thing that's different in our time. Society has changed a lot too. For example, it's perfectly legal and acceptable for two people of the same sex to marry."

Jago and Nathaniel both stiffen up and look at Joanna with wide eyes. I blink in surprise and ask, "What does that have to do with anything?"

No one answers me. Then Jago asks me, "Is this true?"

"Well, yeah," I say. "Only I really don't get what it has to do with anything."

Jago's beard twitches. I think he's smiling, but I have no clue why.

"What's the deal here?" I ask. "One moment we're talking about destroying the Void and now we're discussing gay marriage. I'm sorry, but I fail to see the connection."

Joanna rolls her eyes and sighs, "Oh Zircon."

"What Oh Zircon?" I ask. "It wasn't me who started about romance!"

"I'll explain when we're home," says Joanna.

"Which will be soon," Jago adds with a grin so wide that for the first time his beard hairs part far enough to expose his lips and teeth. "What is your plan, Gwithyas?"

"Ah yes. The plan." I'm still pondering the inexplicable conversation leap from Koeg-killing to wedded bliss, but I suppose that this isn't the best time to discuss the intricacies of human interaction. Joanna, Jago and Nathaniel are all watching me expectantly. It's flattering that they have so much confidence in me, but I'm not sure it's justified. I move the zircon from one hand to the other and back.

"I spoke to Graham," I say. "Just before . . ." I glance apologetically at Nathaniel.

"Just before my rabid attack on you," he finishes my sentence. "There is no need to dodge the subject. We cannot afford such sensitivities at this moment." There's a glimmer in his eyes when he continues, "However, once we're out of here you're under no obligation to ever mention it again."

He smiles. I smile back, glad that he seems to be returning to his usual upbeat self.

Jago asks, "How did you manage to speak to Graham?"

"With this." I hold the zircon up. "I'm not sure how it works, but I when I fell asleep holding this, I got to meet up with the old loony himself. He wasn't so bad, actually. He seemed sorry for what he'd done and willing to end it. He didn't know how to control the Koeg, but he did say that he surrendered the Void and the Koeg and all that to me so I could do with it whatever I need to do, and I think it's all in here."

Everyone glares at the diminutive stone in my palm.

"How?" asks Joanna sceptically. "It's just a stone."

"Yeah," I say, but I'm not really paying attention to Joanna's words. The zircon has started to shimmer, and through the shimmers I can see shapes. I concentrate on the shapes. I have the feeling I should know what they are.

Since I fail to come up with an explanation, Jago takes over. His words trickle into my consciousness while I continue to glare into the orange glow.

"The old magic requires structure," he says. "It is customary to use a solid piece of the Earth itself, like a stone, to bind the magic. And it works best when the binding object has meaning for the witch or warlock. This gem had meaning for Graham Gwithyas."

"Because it belonged to Sophie," I mumble, and Sophie's face, smiling, so obviously a memory from before the Koeg, appears in the zircon.

"Sophie?" ask Joanna and Nathaniel in sync.

"Graham's wife," I say. "He loved her more than anything, he wanted to be the perfect husband, to give her everything a woman could ever wish for. When he discovered that he could do magic, he thought he had found a way."

Sophie's face in the zircon changes from happy to tormented and wet with tears, the way she had looked right before the Koeg killed her. And then she is dead, pale, lifeless. A skull in the fireplace. Tears roll over my cheeks.

"How wrong he was. Sophie didn't want wealth, or power. All she wanted was a happy family life. And Graham destroyed it."

"I think you may be taking this a tad too personal, Zircon," remarks Joanna.

"Let him," says Jago.

I say nothing. I am totally focused on what I see in the zircon, in Graham's mind. I see the Koeg with their horrid, malformed excuses for faces and bodies. And I see the Void, and I see the doorway. Then I look deeper, through the Koeg and the Void and the door, until I see what they really are. Magic, waiting to be changed by mere thought. But I also see the rage, the greed, and Graham's insanity singing through the magic, ready to destroy whatever opposes it. Ready to kill. I turn away. Joanna gives me an inquisitive look.

"What was that about?"

"I saw it," I say. "I know how to do it."

"Do you know how to get us out of here?" asks Joanna, at the same moment as Nathaniel asks, "Do you know how to lock the Void?"

"I think so," I say. "At least, I think I know how it ought to be done. But I can't guarantee it'll work. I might mess it up and make matters worse. And more importantly," I look up, scanning their hopeful faces. "I can't guarantee that any of us will survive."

No one says anything. If Void time wasn't so utterly unreliable I'd say it's about three minutes before someone speaks. That someone is Joanna. She lays her hand on mine and says, "You're the Guardian, Zircon. You'll do it. It's your destiny. And you're not alone, because I am your shield. That is my destiny. I'll be at your side, no matter what."

Nathaniel nods at me. "I too shall stand by you."

"And I," says Jago. "Tell us what needs to be done."

"Well," I say, "I reckon we first need to distract Cecilia. And possibly my uncle. They are not Graham's creations. They're actually human, even if they don't exactly look it any more, so I cannot control them. Plus, they rule the Koeg. Especially Cecilia. She's at least as mad as Graham, but she's not stupid. And she likes to kill."

Nathaniel grimaces as if he is in anguish.

"I'm sorry," I say.

He shakes his head. "Don't be. It is true. I don't know why she has become that way. I have asked myself that so often. She was only a child." He looks me in the eyes. "If you succeed, will Cecilia return to the real world?"

I avert my gaze. "I don't know," I say. I'm not lying. I don't know with full certainty what will happen to Cecilia, or to my uncle Ronald, but I'm pretty sure they'll go down with the Void. I'm just too wimpy to say this to Nathaniel.

"She will not, Nathaniel," Jago says quietly. "You know that. She has changed too much, and she used the magic in the Void to transform herself. She lost her humanity when she did this. When the door closes forever, Cecilia will remain here."

"Is that your opinion too, Gwithyas?" Nathaniel asks.

I fidget with my zircon. "Yeah. I can't be sure, but yeah, I think it's as Jago says."

Nathaniel takes a deep breath. "I lost my sister a long time ago," he says. "You have my full support."

"Sister?" gasps Joanna.

I quickly explain the Gwithyas family's blood connection with the queen of the Koeg. Joanna's eyes widen. She looks from Nathaniel to me and back and rounds her lips. Before she manages to make an awkward remark I say, "So I was thinking if I can distract Cecilia enough to let the doorway open without her noticing, you lot can go through."

"I'll distract her," says Nathaniel. "I know her, I know how to get her attention."

"Why are we going through and not you?" asks Joanna. "I'm not going anywhere without you."

"And what about the Koeg?" asks Jago. "There are always a few on guard in case the doorway opens. They'll dash through as soon as they spot the tiniest gap."

"Yeah," I say. "I know. That's why you'll have to go through. If I were to go first, the Koeg would be all over me before I could do anything. So you lot have to fight them. Joanna, your sword and Nathaniel's dagger are the only things that can hold the Koeg back. Jago, you can fight too, can't you? I saw you whack an axe about when the Koeg were attacking me. Use that axe. We'll need all the combat power we have. Once you are all on the other side, I'll follow."

"And so will a complete gang of Koeg," comments Joanna. "What's the point of that? Why not kill them while we are in here?"

"I can't," I explain. "In here I can only do a little magic. Not enough to get rid of the Koeg, but once I'm on real, solid ground I'll tap directly into the powers of the hill, and if I understood everything right that should make me a lot more powerful, and enable me to re-shape Graham's creations. I should easily be strong enough to lock the door forever."

Jago's eyebrows knit together into a single bristle. "It could work," he says. "Indeed, it could very well work."

"It could also be an epic fail," I point out. "In which case we will all die horrible, painful deaths and we'll unleash the Koeg's evil into the real world. But if we do nothing, that will happen anyway. So we don't really have a choice."

Joanna frowns. "I still don't like the idea of you staying behind here on your own, Zircon."

"We have no choice," I repeat. "Think of it this way: the people most likely to die in this set-up are you three. I'll remain outside the physical battle. Compared to you lot, I'll be as safe as if I were in a Buddhist monastery."

Joanna sighs. "Yeah, I suppose. So, when do we start?"

"How about right now?"

We all twist around as Cecilia's voice fills the room. It's not just her voice that fills the room. Cecilia herself is a lot bigger than usual and takes up all the space behind us, and she also fills the air with putrid fumes that make my stomach turn. She's decaying. Her flesh is sliding from her body in festering lumps. It doesn't seem to bother her much, because she grins at me and doesn't even wince when a couple of teeth fall from her rotting gums. "Hello, Gwithyas. Getting a bit overconfident, are you? Don't worry. We are here to fix your delusions."

She grabs my head between her hands, now fat clumps of spongy flesh with crooked fingers, and presses her long fingernails into my temples.

"We'll get through that doorway, Gwithyas. If we need to crack your skull to do it, we will. You haven't felt a proper headache yet."

"And he won't," shouts Joanna.

Her sword flashes an inch away from my nose. Cecilia wails as her severed claws land on the floor with two sickening thuds. A cloud of blood mists my glasses over. I rub them clean and when my vision is clear again I see handless Cecilia, shaking her head in dismay. "So unkind," she complains. "And I thought we could be friends."

She raises her arms, splashing blood everywhere, and Koeg start sprouting from her bloody stumps. One, two, six… too many to count.

Joanna and Nathaniel crash into action. Their weapons move so fast that they are nothing but vibrating smudges. I can't see Jago, but I hear him grunt as he too attacks the monsters. But there are so many Koeg, and Cecilia keeps producing more. Joanna, Nathaniel and Jago cannot possibly fend them all off. So much for our plan. I start scrambling up, not thinking, just wanting to help, but then Uncle Ronald appears in front of me and digs a razor-claw into my skull.

"Hello little nephew," he growls.

Something tears in my brain and I lose control of my body. My arms and legs spasm as if I'm having a seizure. I cry out, from fear more than pain. Uncle Ronald drags me up, dangles me in front of his face and studies me. My muscles are jerking violently.

"You thought you could control the Void," says Uncle Ronald, "But look at you. You cannot even control your own limbs."

Cecilia peeks over his shoulder and waves her arm stumps at her mouth. She has something between her teeth, something orange and shiny. The zircon. But how? Uncle Ronald tuts. "You dropped it, nephew. You're such a stupid stupid boy."

The door materialises right next to Cecilia. She aims the gem at it and pushes the door open with her mutilated arms.

"See, Gwithyas?" sniggers Uncle Ronald, "We can do it ourselves. Told you."

My mind cracks into blinding agony as the door starts to open. I feel blood trickle inside my head and then out of my nose, and as it oozes over my mouth, the door opens wider. For a brief moment I glimpse the sky of the real world, but that view is soon obscured by waves of Koeg tumbling through the doorway.

"Gwithyas!" Two strong arms embrace me. Jago. He is clutching my convulsing body and shouts, "I got him!"

And then there is Joanna. Roaring like a berserk Viking she dashes through a crowd of misshapen atrocities, waving her sword, dismembering Koeg as she goes, catapulting their severed body parts off her blade. Before the Koeg have the time to react Joanna has slashed Ronald in two, and when his writhing top half plummets down next to me I can move again. Jago lets go of me.

Cecilia is still at the door with the gem, but the door is now at the end of a long corridor, much further away than before. She places one foot on the doorstep. I start running, but I know it's pointless. She's too far and I've never been much of a sportsman. But someone else is, and he rushes past me. Nathaniel.

"Cecilia!" he bellows. "Stop that at once!"

It works. Cecilia freezes on the spot and turns to face her brother. Her eyes whirl as if they consist of greasy smoke and she hisses. Nathaniel slows down, but he doesn't stop. "You're a very naughty girl, Cecilia," he shouts, and he actually waves a finger at her, which strikes me as a ridiculously inappropriate and inadequate thing to do to a giant rotting corpse with a murderous attitude. And yet, it works. Cecilia's eyes smoke more fiercely, and her full focus is now on Nathaniel instead of on the door. She growls at him, a deep, thundering growl that shakes my bones. Nathaniel keeps going.

"Step away from that door right now!" he orders, and that's too much for his putrefying sibling.

"You are not the boss of me!" shrieks Cecilia as she pounces at her brother. The zircon is launched from between her jaws and lands so close to me that I only need to pick it up. I seal my fingers around the gem—and around two or three of Cecilia's dislodged teeth. The door is almost completely open and Nathaniel and Cecilia, locked in a bloody struggle, tumble through, followed by swarms of Koeg. There must be hundreds of them in the real world now, no doubt destroying everything and everyone they encounter.

"Follow them!" I cry. "Joanna! Jago! Follow them and kill them!"

Jago leaps to the other side, piercing a thin Koeg on his dagger, but Joanna hesitates.

"Go!" I shout at her. "Go! Go! GO!"

"Not without you," she says. She grabs my hand and drags me through the doorway, and we fly amongst hordes of elated Koeg, out of the Void into the garden of the manor.

Joanna's hand slips from mine. She rolls over her shoulder, leaps to her feet and immediately starts lashing out at the Koeg. I land a few feet away from her in a much less impressive fashion, bottom first. I scramble up as fast as I can. Koeg are everywhere, emitting noises that grate on my eardrums, and judging from the sweltering heat and dense smoke around me the critters have taken up pyromania. It doesn't bother me. I'm not even scared. I feel something else, not an emotion but a titillating sensation that unfolds under my skin, travels up through my feet, my legs, my stomach, to gather in my left fist into a dense clump of power. I know what this is. It's the magic of the hill.

A small spiny Koeg soars towards me, clearly with violent intentions. With a quick thought I turn it into a paper air plane. I giggle. This is fun. Another Koeg spouts acid at me but I mirror the stuff back and make the Koeg explode in a shower of mayonnaise. I'm burning, but in a good way, not with fire or fever, but with powerful magic that penetrates every atom of my body. I know it does this because I can sense each individual atom as well as the forces that connect them, and the forces that connect me to the Earth. I possess the power and the solidity of the entire planet, and I can shape it into anything I desire. Nothing could possibly harm me.

A third Koeg becomes a bouncy rubber ball and a fourth a pair of socks. I'm laughing out loud. Then Joanna calls out. She's clearly not having as much fun as me. In fact she sounds terrified, verging on the hysterical. "Zircon! There are too many! We can't hold them back and they're attacking the town!"

I look down the hill. Plumes of dark smoke rise from the town. The church tower is ablaze and people are scurrying over the steaming streets in an erratic fashion, trying to save their hides. As I watch, a yellow shop sign shoots up in a flash of fire. It's the sign of the fish'n'chips outlet where those cool kids gathered—the kids that made fun of me. I wonder if they were there when the Koeg attacked. If they were, they are now probably a very uncool mass of minced body parts. I don't like that idea. They may have been bullies, but no one deserves an end like that. Besides, Joanna probably knew them.

Another explosion, closer this time, exactly at the bottom of the hill. Must be the video library. I don't think the spotty guy who works there ever leaves his shop, so he's dead for sure. This can't go on. The time for bouncy balls and paper planes is over. Joanna confirms that conclusion by screaming at me, "Zircon Gwithyas! Do something! Nathaniel is down and Jago and I can't keep going!"

I glance over the burning grass of what used to be our garden. There's Joanna, slashing apart one Koeg after another. Jago is chopping a cluster of scaly atrocities to bits with his axe. Nathaniel is lying on the grass near the fence. His left trouser leg is drenched with blood, but he's leaning on one arm and still stabs his dagger at the multitude of Koeg that keep coming at him.

I observe it all as if it were a bad action film. I know ought to be devastated and horrified, but I am not. I feel strangely calm.

"Keep fighting!" I shout at Joanna. "Distract them and keep them away from me. I have to think."

"Think?" she shrieks back. "Better think really really fast then!"

She sounds angry but she hacks her sword into the Koeg with renewed vigour, making sure the Koeg get no chance to come near me. I concentrate on my thoughts, trying to think how to resolve the current situation. Damn Cecilia. If she hadn't attacked I would've had the chance to figure all this out in advance. Jago could've helped me, because he knows about these things. But he did say something, didn't he? Or no, it was in the instructions. Yes, that was it: '*It is the ritual that channels the magic.*' And what did the ritual do again? It shut the door. So that's it. I'll have to chant the spell to close the door. But there's a hitch. When I look around but can't see the door anywhere. That is ridiculous, I came through it only moments ago. It can't be gone. It probably zapped to another place, like everything in the Void always seems to do. So I look again, and this time I spot the door, almost completely obscured by the fire and smoke that rises from burning trees, in the wall of the tower, all the way up where Nanny's room was. Or still is, because in the doorway stands Nanny, seemingly not at all disturbed by the Koeg that soar past her into my world. She is looking at me with an expression that I've never seen on her face before. At least not directed at me. I think it might be admiration, because she says, "You can do more than close the door, young warlock. You have the ability to end this forever."

She opens her hands, releasing two orange lights that flutter through the fire and the smoke and then turn into my sisters. They are a little translucent but seem otherwise fine.

"You're a bit of a surprise, big brother," says Amethyst.

"Young descendant," Opal corrects her. "But she's right. We have never witnessed powers like yours. Even Nanny was impressed. That's why she composed you a new spell."

"New spell?" I ask. "What are you talking about? I don't have the time to learn a new spell! The town is being decimated, Joanna and Jago are at the ends of their tether and Nathaniel . . ." I peer to the far end of the garden. Nathaniel is lying motionless in the grass, face down. " . . .has just passed out," I finish my sentence. "Or he is dead. I have to act now. There's no time for occult poetry."

"Don't fret," says Opal. "Just repeat after us. It's only short."

"But . . ."

Amethyst interrupts me. "No time for arguments, you said so yourself."

"What will happen to the two of you?" I ask. "Will you die too? Will you be gone forever? And Nanny?"

"We're already dead," says Opal. "So we won't die again. Whether our souls will still be around or not is entirely up to you. As for Nanny—if you succeed, she will finally be at peace. Now stop talking and listen."

There is a massive explosion in town, so loud that it reverberates in my chest. I dare not turn around to see what has happened, but the blast is a stern reminder of the urgency of the situation, so I listen as Amethyst explains the procedure.

"You need to imagine that you send the Koeg back and then destroy the Void. Your imagination will become reality, just like it did earlier, when you turned those Koeg into household objects. Use the gem as your focus. Its solidity will channel your power and allow you to work on the whole of Graham's creation. The words will shape the magic. Just repeat what we say."

I'm not convinced. I think it may be better to just stick with what I've already done and use the old spell to close the door. But my sisters appear so confident.

"You sure?" I ask nervously.

"Very," insist my sisters.

Another explosion. No time for negotiating. I press my palms over the zircon and close my eyes. "It'll be fine," I mutter to myself. "The Koeg are not real, after all. Creatures of the mind. This should be a breeze."

As it turns out, it's more like a tornado. The Koeg may be immaterial, but they certainly have their own desires, and those don't include travelling via my cortex into oblivion. As soon as I repeat Opal and Amethyst's first words all the Koeg come rushing at me, shrieking and lashing out. For once I am grateful for my poor vision; if I hadn't been wearing glasses the Koeg would've ripped my eyeballs out. I press my palms together so hard that the zircon cuts into my skin and I shout out the new spell:

Gorfenna Browagh
Ladha Dyowlow
Daras Klos
Drog Gyllys

The Koeg squirm as they are all pressed into something that resembles a horizontal whirlwind, and then they are sucked into my head like the starship Voyager into a wormhole. The force of their involuntary withdrawal is so colossal that it ought to have squashed me, but it doesn't. I stay upright with my feet firmly planted on the ground while the old magic flows through me, empowering me until I sort of feel like Superman. Not like his Clark Kent guise either, no, the real thing with super-strength and x-ray eyes or whatever. I even think I could fly if I wanted to. My skin is warm, my body strong, and my mind stable and uncompromising. I feel better than I have ever done in my entire life. Obliterating monsters suits me.

I stand there grinning while the Koeg hurl through me, faster and faster, so fast that I lose track of what is happening. Someone grabs my arm. Joanna? But the hollow sockets that hover in front of my face are not almond shaped. They're emitting an almost tangible rage. This has to be Cecilia. She seems to have given up on maintaining any kind of physical coherence and her voice rumbles at me from a blob of gangrenous flesh. "Don't do this! I am your family. You cannot condemn me to an everlasting non-existence!"

I don't bother to reply. She knows very well that I intend to do exactly that.

"Please!" gargles Cecilia, and then she is gone. And so am I.

I'm nowhere. There is no ground under my feet, and the space around me isn't even dark. Or space, for that matter. There is nothing. I'm not worried though. I understand. This utter emptiness must be the original Void. The Koeg, the fake manor and all of Jago's objects have ceased to exist. Or not? I hear something. That can't be right; there shouldn't be anything here. I use my magic to think the sound into sight, but regret doing that as soon as I spot two pulsating grey eyeballs in a puddle of bloody intestines, both looking awfully familiar. I look closer, not at the guts, mind you, those eyeballs on their own are sickening enough. They look like my father's eyes, but not quite.

"Uncle Ronald?" I ask cautiously.

There is no answer, only some quiet squelching.

"I'm sorry," I say to the eyes. "I would've preferred to take you home and have you admitted to a psychiatric institution or something. After all, you are my only living relative." I tap a finger to my mouth as a thought occurs to me. "Actually, that's not true," I say. "You're not really living for one, and I now have Jago and Nathaniel. They are my family too."

The eyes look a bit disgruntled.

"Isn't it great?" I cheer. "The Void did some good after all. Even though centuries passed in the real world, Jago and Nathaniel only spent a few years of their lives in there, and they can now continue to live in my time. I wonder what they'll make of the digital age." Then I have another thought. I smile widely at the eyes. "And Joanna! She's supposed to become my wife, remember? If a wife is not a close relative than I don't know who is. Sorry Uncle Ronald, but I don't need you."

The pupils widen, and then the eyes grow blurry. I turn away from them and look around. Or I try, but since there is not really anything that qualifies as 'around' I just look. I need to get out of here. I need the door. The zircon, which is still in my hand, warms and turns into a doorknob. How convenient.

I turn back to the eyes, but they're gone. I guess they were only there because I wanted them to be, because I still needed to feel like I had a living relative. I could've chosen a less distasteful form though. I decide that from now on I shall think things through before doing magic.

I step through the doorway.

CHAPTER 17
Life

I'M NO LONGER STANDING. I'M LYING ON MY BACK IN MY CHARACteristic sprawl-over-the-ground position and the magic drizzles out of my body until I am my flimsy self again. The zircon is still in my hand, and I stick it unceremoniously in my pocket before standing up.

It's dark. I have no idea if that is because it's night, or because the smoke that I smell all around me is so dense that it blocks the light of the sun. It doesn't matter. The effect is the same: I can't see anything but some crude outlines of what I presume to be the remnants of my parental home. It is often said that if one sense fails you, you use another. So I stand motionless and I listen. It's quiet now that the Koeg are all gone, but not soundless. I hear the crackling of smouldering wood, and in the distance the cries of horror-struck townsfolk. I also hear footsteps. They patter rapidly over the ground and come to a halt immediately in front of me.

"Zircon!"

"Joanna."

"Where did they go?"

I tap on my head. "In here. Are you okay?"

"I-in . . ." stammers Joanna. "Yes, I am okay. Are you telling me that the Koeg went into your head?"

"Sort of," I say. "They were creatures of the mind after all. It was about time they started to behave like it."

Joanna places a finger on my forehead. "And that is safe?"

I'm slightly insulted by her obvious lack of trust. I mean, I just defeated an entire army of brutal living hallucinations. Surely some admiration would've been in place.

"It's perfectly safe," I snort. "They are now as immaterial as those glamorous heroic guardians in *your* mind."

"Sorry," says Joanna. "I didn't mean to sound unconvinced."

"I'm used to it," I say, sounding a little more embittered than I intended. Better change the subject. "Where are the others?"

"They're right over there."

"Yeah," I say, gazing in what I hope is the direction she's pointing.

"You lost your glasses again, didn't you?" asks Joanna.

"No. I didn't *lose* them as such. Those glasses were made in the Void, so they disappeared along with the Koeg. How are they? I mean Jago and Nathaniel, not my glasses."

"Nathaniel is badly hurt," says Joanna. "Jago has stopped the bleeding for now, but we need to get Nat to a hospital as soon as possible. You don't happen to have a phone on you, do you?"

I am a little taken aback by this question. I mean, after all that happened Joanna asks whether I have a phone on me. As if we've gone for a pleasant hike in the hills instead of getting stuck in the magical realm of someone else's materialised nightmare, and nearly dying there.

"Well?" asks Joanna, "Do you have one?"

"No."

"Didn't think so. In that case you and I will need to walk to town to get help."

"Yes," I say, and I stretch my back in preparation for the walk.

"Yes," says Joanna, but she doesn't move.

"Well?" I ask.

"You saved the world," says Joanna.

She flings her arms around my neck and kisses me. It's so

sudden that I don't immediately register what is going on, and I stand there like a poorly constructed scarecrow. Joanna keeps her lips firmly pressed on mine until I relax, fold my arms around her waist and return her kiss. Just before I shut my eyes I see two orange sparks flicker in the dark.

About The Author

ISHA CROWE IS A QUAINT MIDDLE-AGED HOUSEWIFE WHO LIVES IN a quaint old seaside town, and whose hobbies include watching 'Flog It' on TV, serving her two cats, baking cakes, gardening, and dreaming up grisly stories about weird folk in surreal situations.

She's worked in childcare for thirty-odd years, but has been writing since she was able to control a pen. Her very first stories focused on kittens and puppies and were written in Dutch, her first language.

Isha grew up in Suriname, became an adult in the Netherlands, ripened in Cornwall and now lives in Wales amongst dragons and daffodils.

She blogs at ishacrowe.wordpress.com and can also be found on Facebook.

A Selection of Other Titles from Kristell Ink

Green Sky & Sparks by Kate Coe

In a world of magic, wind, and electricity, Catter Jeck is offered the chance to explore a myth. Travelling from city to city, his search for the centre of the magic catches others in its coils. When the Lord Heir of Meton offers to continue the search in his flying machine, the consequences of their crash—and Toru's accidental link to a dying Healer—suddenly become of central importance to all of their lives.

Fear the Reaper by Tom Lloyd

All Shell has ever wanted was a home, a place to belong. But now an angel of the God has tracked her down, intent on using her to hunt the demon that once saved her. The journey will take her into the dead place beyond the borders of the world, there to face her past and witness the coming of a new age.

A stand-alone novella from the author of The Twilight Reign series and Moon's Artifice.

Atlantis & The Game of Time by K.M Alford

Their goal is a single culture, a single history, threatening to obliterate all others, with peace forged only through oppression.

From the dingy annals of human prehistory, a new culture emerges. Like the Atlantians, they too can travel through time, but these are no passive, desk-soft anthropologists, and they will not be satisfied with coexistence. They desire to absorb, to assimilate, and will crush any civilisation that stands against them. The Atlantians know the price of complicity is too high; they will not risk the annihilation of human advancement, culture, art, and freedom. Instead, they send their overworked operative, Professor Lokyne, and a select group of book-loving, academic activists to face this new enemy. Atlantis's only hope is that they can employ their research and cultural integration skills to study their new enemy, find a weakness, and then strike from within. Only then can they hope to bring down this parasitic new civilisation and return the flow of time to its normal course.

In this fast-paced, exquisitely detailed adventure, we follow the trepidatious group as it struggles across time and culture from ancient Egypt and Babylon, to China and beyond, exploring equality and the injustice inherent when one culture seeks to extinguish another.

www.kristell-ink.com

Lightning Source UK Ltd.
Milton Keynes UK
UKOW01f0756270218
318508UK00001B/3/P

9 781911 497349